King of the Trenches 2

Lock Down Publications and Ca$h
Presents
King of the Trenches 2
A Novel by *Ghost & Tranay Adams*

Lock Down Publications
Po Box 944
Stockbridge, Ga 30281

Visit our website @
www.lockdownpublications.com

Lock Down Publications
Like our page on Facebook: Lock Down Publications @
www.facebook.com/lockdownpublications.ldp
Book interior design by: **Shawn Walker**
Edited by: **Shamika Smith**

Stay Connected with Us!

Text **LOCKDOWN** to 22828 to stay up-to-date with new releases, sneak peaks, contests and more…
Thank you.

Submission Guideline.

Submit the first three chapters of your completed manuscript to ldpsubmissions@gmail.com, subject line: Your book's title. The manuscript must be in a .doc file and sent as an attachment. Document should be in Times New Roman, double spaced and in size 12 font. Also, provide your synopsis and full contact information. If sending multiple submissions, they must each be in a separate email.

Have a story but no way to send it electronically? You can still submit to LDP/Ca$h Presents. Send in the first three chapters, written or typed, of your completed manuscript to:

LDP: Submissions Dept
Po Box 944
Stockbridge, Ga 30281

DO NOT send original manuscript. Must be a duplicate.

Provide your synopsis and a cover letter containing your full contact information.

Thanks for considering LDP and Ca$h Presents.

Ghost & Tranay Adams

Chapter 1

Now that Jabari had sent Ramone away on his mission, it was time he tied up a loose end. His mind switched to the heated discussion between him and Jayshawn. He had mad love for him and Ramone and sort of looked at them like extended family, but all of that was about to change. Jayshawn had him fucked up on so many levels for thinking he could talk to a nigga of his caliber the way he had. He was known as a big stepper throughout Brooklyn. His opps feared and respected him. He'd locked ass with some of the most reputable killas to have ever touched a New York City block, so he'd be damned if he let some dusty, bum-ass nigga talk to him like he didn't dance with wolves and bust his gun.

Jabari was a cold-blooded hitta, and he felt like Jayshawn had forgotten about that. That was okay, though, because he was on his way to give his ass a reminder.

Jabari drove his Dodge Charger up his driveway and inside of his garage. As the garage door was closing behind him, he was hopping out of the car and slamming the door shut. He stripped down to his wife-beater and boxer briefs and stepped into a black and red leather motorcycle suit. He laced his boots, put on his gloves, and drew a large plastic knife he'd forged for this very mission from its hiding place. Jabari approached the beige bust of a rubber mannequin standing up against the wall. He took a professional stance with his knife at his side and swiftly stabbed the left side of its torso four times. The blade went through the dummy quite easily, so he knew he wouldn't have any trouble putting it through Jayshawn.

Jabari snatched off one of his gloves and pressed his thumb against the tip of the plastic knife. Blood oozed into the form of a dot on his thumb. Sucking his thumb, he smiled wickedly and nodded with the satisfaction of his fine-crafted weapon. He pulled his glove back over his hand and flexed his fingers inside of it. He unzipped his motorcycle suit and sheathed his plastic knife inside of it. He pocketed a white Coronavirus mask, pulled his motorcycle helmet over his head, and climbed onto his Ducati Super Sport. Kicking up its kickstand, he turned on his bike and revved it up. The motorcycle whined loudly and annoyingly.

Jabari pressed the button on the wall that activated the garage door. As soon as the door lifted up, he revved up his Ducati again and zipped down the driveway. He made a right onto the paved residential street and zipped up the boulevard. He popped a wheelie halfway down the road, came down, and zipped up the block faster. A moment later, the red taillight of his bike disappeared into the darkness like an apparition.

Jabari parked his Ducati in a nearby alley. He camouflaged it underneath cardboard, old newspapers, black garbage bags, and a few other items littering the path. Still in his helmet, he walked across the street and made his way onto hospital grounds. The security guard was asleep at the front desk with his cap pulled low over his brows, so he didn't prove a problem getting by.

Jabari was walking down the elevator lobby when he noticed one of the hospital's janitors. He was a fiftyish white man wearing a cap, a Coronavirus mask, and Dickie jumpsuit. He was pushing his cleaning cart onto an elevator car that had just arrived. Jabari looked at the up and down buttons on the panel. The up button was lit, so he knew he was going up. The elevator's doors were almost closed until he stuck his gloved hand between them. They reopened, and he stepped inside. He exchanged nods with the janitor and pressed the number to the floor he desired.

Jabari posted up at the back of the elevator and opened his helmet's visor. He examined the janitor closely, figuring they wore about the same size in clothing and shoes. Glancing at the numbers they'd selected on the panel, he noticed they had a few stops left before they reached the floor he'd personally selected. With that in mind, he made his move swiftly. He slipped up behind the older man and applied the Sleeper Hold to him. The man gritted and struggled to break the hold.

"Shhhhhhh. Relax, Pops. You look like you could use a nap," Jabari told him. Seconds later, his movements slowed and he'd fallen asleep, snoring. Jabari laid him down inside of the elevator and pressed the emergency stop button. He removed his helmet, unzipped his leather suit, and began getting dressed in his victim's uniform.

***

The elevator doors opened. Jabari rolled out the cleaning cart wearing the Coronavirus mask and his cap pulled low. He left the janitor slumped against the elevator wall wearing his helmet and motorcycle suit. Jabari was halfway down the hall-way to Jayshawn's room by the time the elevator's doors closed. The window of opportunity was closing fast. He knew it was only a matter of time before the janitor was discovered inside of the elevator and the staff came looking for answers. He wanted to make Jayshawn's death bloody and extremely painful, but time wouldn't permit it. He'd have to alternate and settle for quick and clean.

Jabari stopped his cleaning cart at Jayshawn's hospital door. He looked up and down the hallway. The few staff members that were around weren't paying any attention to him. They were too busy talking among themselves and completing tasks. The Delta variant of the Coronavirus was taking over the city of New York like crazy. There were patients storming into the hospital ten and twenty at a time to the point that the medical building was at capacity. Jabari grew confident that he'd be able to take care of business without being accosted. He slipped into the room and softly closed the door behind himself.

Jabari stole a look inside of the dark room. Jayshawn was lying in bed asleep with the glow of the television's screen dancing across his face.

Jabari pulled his plastic knife from inside his Dickie jumpsuit, gripping it like Michael Myers and creeping up on Jayshawn's bedside.

This is going to be like taking candy from a baby, he thought as sweat rolled down his back. Jayshawn tossed and turned in bed. Every movement he made in bed caused Jabari to become angrier and angrier until his chest heaved up and down.

Jayshawn pulled the covers over his body and closed his eyes, lying flat on his back. The morphine that they were pumping into his body had him feeling as if he were in another world. He smiled and shook his head a few times, before sighing. *Damn, I don't wanna get hooked on this shit,* he thought. *Every nigga in the Apple hooked on shit like this and I see why, but the god ain't going, fuck that.* He stretched his legs out and cracked his toes before smacking his lips together loudly.

Jabari eased closer to the bed, ready to slam the knife downward like a maniacal serial killer. With every step that he got closer to Jayshawn, the hatred that flowed deep within him seemed to bubble to the surface. Finally, he stood over him with a serious mug of fury written across his face. The scent from the Janitor's cologne plagued his nostrils. He leaned over Jayshawn and meticulously placed the ridges of the homemade plastic knife just above Jayshawn's jugular and then with extreme precision, he sliced his neck, causing blood to skeet across the room. Before the injury could take effect on Jayshawn, he sliced him again, and blood spurted on the television's screen.

In a morphine-induced haze, Jayshawn was slow to react, but suddenly the pain of the attack broke through the supposed numbness of the drug. He slapped his right hand to the gash and sat up with blood dripping from his fingers. His eyes were bucked open so wide that they looked as if they were seconds away from popping out of his face.

"Yeah, bitch-ass nigga, I told you I was gon' catch you lacking. This shit ain't over until I slump yo' chump ass," Jabari hissed.

Jayshawn hopped out of the bed with blood squirting all over the room. "What the fuck, nigga?" He staggered on his feet, still holding his neck. "You got me, dawg. It's over."

Jabari hopped over the bed. "Nah, nigga, it ain't over until I say it's over." He slammed the knife into Jayshawn's stomach and ripped it upward before he punched him as hard as he could directly into the incision that he'd just made.

"Oof!" Jayshawn fell to his knees with his eyes closed. He reached up for Jabari with little strength. He scratched him across the face.

"Ahhhh!" Jabari kicked Jayshawn in the chest as hard as he could, sending him up under the hospital bed. "Get the fuck up off of me!"

Jayshawn slid under the bed. He began to shake uncontrollably. Reddish white foam began to fizz out of the side of his mouth. He rolled on to his side and came to a pushup position in an attempt to get up. Jabari hustled over and sat on his back. He pulled his head toward him by use of his forehead and sliced his throat three quick times before slamming his face so hard into the linoleum that it shattered his facial bones, causing his mug to sink inward. He stood up and kicked him as hard as he could in the ribs. There were two knocks on the door. "Jayshawn, it's Nurse Kelly, are you decent?" she asked, just opening the door a peek.

Jabari hopped back with his heart pounding in his chest. "Fuck, what do I do?" he asked himself, looking over at Jayshawn and watching the puddle of blood form around his remains. He rushed to the side of the door and cleared his throat. "Fuck."

"Jayshawn, did you hear what I asked you?" the short, heavyset, black woman asked with her weave braids flowing down her back.

Jabari began to shake. "Uh, yeah, I'm decent, Miss Kelly."

"Good, because I think we're going to have to discharge you because the hospital is at capac——" She opened the door all the way and saw that the room looked like a scene out of a scary movie. She screamed at the top of her lungs.

Jabari flashed in front of her and sliced her throat. "Bitch, shut up." Then he took off running through the hospital toward his escape, forcing people out of his way again and again.

Nurse Kelly fell to her knees holding her throat, and then her side. She reached up for anything, but nothing was close enough for her to grab on too. She rolled onto her stomach and willed herself to her feet. Once there, she staggered to the front desk and collapsed in front of her coworkers. They went into a frenzy in an effort to help her recover.

Chapter 2

The Chevrolet Tahoe sat idling in the alley three houses down from Olivia's crib. M.O.P's "Ante up" was pumping so loudly from its speakers that the entire truck was vibrating. The SUV was filled with smoke as Boobie and Durty were passing a blunt of Jamaica's finest between them while Ramone tooted coke up his nose in the backseat. Ramone snorted up the last of the cocaine from his fist and threw his head back. "Wooooo!" he shouted like Ric Flair, looking around and blinking his teary eyes. He then snorted like a warthog, dug in his nose, and then pulled on it.

Boobie passed the blunt to Durty. He adjusted the rearview mirror and looked up into it. He was so startled by Ramone's demonic appearance that he clutched his gun tighter.

"Blood, what the fucks up wit'chu?" Durty asked off of his reaction. Boobie threw his head toward the backseat. Durty looked over his shoulder and was taken aback by Ramone's terrifying appearance as well. The young nigga looked like a crazed psychopath. "Yo, you good, son?"

"Yeah, yeah, I'm good, Dunn. I'm just ready to drill some shit, ya heard?" Ramone slipped on his black sunglasses, threw his hood over his head, and whipped out his black leather gloves. "Yo, crank that shit up. I'm getting in my zone."

Ramone pulled the black leather gloves over his hands as he spat the lyrics to the song. The mixture of cocaine and crunked-up music had him amped up. He cocked the slide on his gun, putting a hollow tip bullet in its chamber. It was now a deadly weapon!

Ramone jumped out of the truck, tucked his piece in his waistband, and made his way towards Olivia's crib with murder on his mind.

***

Paperchase had to link up with Olivia to drop off Scorpion's cut from the moves he'd been making in the streets. He was driving up her block when he saw her pass something concealed in a towel to someone in a white BMW X6 with red-tinted windows. He didn't have a clue as to who the driver was, but he could make out their silhouette through the red-tinted windows of their whip. It was most definitely a woman. A tall one at that. He couldn't tell for sure, but he thought she'd glanced at him in passing.

Paperchase pulled his SRT into Olivia's driveway, killed the engine, and hopped out. She stood on her front porch with her hands folded across her breasts, waiting for him. He popped his trunk open and grabbed a Gucci knapsack from out of it. He slung one of its straps over his shoulder, glanced at his Rollie, and jogged up the short steps that led to the porch.

"Yo, who was shorty that was just over here?" Paperchase asked out of curiosity.

"Why? You jealous?" Olivia grinned. She then pulled him so close to her he could smell the minty toothpaste she'd used to brush her teeth. "If you are, then don't be, Pa, 'cause you're the only nigga Fat Ma gets wet for," she whispered into his ear while cuffing the bulge in his jeans.

"Relax. I already told you what it is from now on between us." Paperchase gently pushed her back. "Now, let's go inside and get this money counted up so you can make sure it gets to bro's offshore account." He brushed past her, heading inside of the house and leaving her on the front porch, looking stupid as fuck. She grinned, licked her top row of teeth, and spun on her heels. She marched inside of the house, shut the door behind her, and locked it.

Paperchase dumped the contents of the Gucci knapsack onto the kitchen table. He pulled out a chair, sat down, and began removing the rubber bands from around the stacks of dead presidents. Olivia rifled through the cupboards and cabinets inside of the kitchen for the money counter. A look of frustration was on her face because she was having trouble finding it, and she was bitching about it under her breath.

"Dónde diablos está esa maldita máquina? Sé que lo puse aquí en alguna parte (Where the fuck is that goddamn machine? I know I put it in here somewhere)," Olivia complained. Suddenly, she stopped rifling through the cabinets and a smile spread across her face. "There you are. I knew I put you somewhere in here." She grabbed the money counter from where it was hidden behind the pots and pans, set it down on the kitchen table, and pulled up a chair.

Paperchase pulled out a half-ounce bag of Purple Kush and began breaking it down on the kitchen table. He knew exactly how much bread he was kicking up to Scorpion, having counted it three times. But every time he made a drop-off to Olivia for her to deposit, he made her count it again in front of him so there wouldn't be any misunderstanding. Although he was putting the pipe to Olivia and he had feelings for her, he wasn't going to let his emotions cloud his judgment. Paperchase knew as well as anyone else that chances were that if the opposite sex or money was involved, circumstances and people changed. He didn't raise a fuss about it. That was just how it was.

Paperchase had smoked a little more than half of his blunt by the time Olivia had finished counting up the money and putting rubber bands back around it. He watched carefully as she reloaded the Gucci knapsack with blue cheese, drew the strings, closed its flap, and then slung its strap over her shoulder. She made her way inside of her bedroom to hide the knapsack until she went to holler at Scorpion's banker tomorrow.

As soon as Olivia was out of his sight, Paperchase mashed out what was left of his blunt and placed it behind his ear. He slipped on his jacket and stashed what was left of the Kush inside of his jacket's pocket. He then snatched up his car keys and walked to the front door. He'd just unlocked the door and pulled it open when Olivia came out of nowhere and pushed it shut.

"And just where do you think you're going, mister?" Olivia asked, grabbing the collar of his jacket and walking him backwards. The only thing she had on now was her bra and panties. She'd been planning to make her move on Paperchase as soon as they were done conducting business.

"I've got business to take care of, Liv. I don't have time to play with yo' ass, so move outta my way," Paperchase said, irritated, shoving her out of his way. He reached for the doorknob, but she grabbed his hand and swung his arm around her waist. She grabbed his other hand and swung it around as well.

She licked his neck over his throat and started sucking the soft flesh below his chin. In the midst of doing this, she slid his strong masculine hands down the small of her back and forcibly made him cuff her buttocks. She licked his lips and sucked on his bottom one, gently pulling on it. She slipped her tongue inside of his mouth. They closed their eyes and started kissing. The sound of their saliva moving inside of their mouths and their moaning filled the living room. Paperchase gripped both of her globes, and the meat of them seeped between his fingers. He began rubbing all over her ass and then groping them like they were a pair of perky titties. Before he knew it, his dick was as hard as a baseball bat, and he was ready to hit something.

Paperchase tilted his head back and closed his eyes, moaning loudly. Olivia bit and sucked on his neck as she helped him out of his clothes. She'd gotten him down to his wifebeater when he started to realize what was happening.

"Stop, stop, stop!" Paperchase pushed her off him. He held up his hand to keep her where she was and used his other hand to wipe her red lipstick kisses off him.

Olivia caught herself before she could fall. She turned around and looked at Paperchase like he'd lost his goddamn mind. "Nigga, what the fuck is wrong with you?"

"Bitch, don't act brand new. I told you what was up when I came over here!" Paperchase spat angrily with his fists clenched at his sides. His face was balled up, and he was gritting his teeth.

To her, he looked so cute when he was mad, especially now that he had the hickies she'd given him running up and down his neck. "Oh, now it's foul, huh? It wasn't foul all the other times we got down," Olivia said as she rose to her pretty feet. She slowly walked toward him, unfastening her bra from the back. Her panties played hide and seek between her ample buttocks with every step she took.

"Well, it is now! And this shit is stopping today!" Paperchase barked and jabbed his finger at her.

"Nigga, you got me fucked up, ain't shit stopping!" Olivia barked back at him and smacked his hand down. She forced him up against the wall and grabbed his semi-erect dick. "You started this shit, and we're not done until I say we're done!" Her nose and lips grazed his as she spoke. Her demanding demeanor and feminine touch aroused him. She was driving him crazy, and he was finding it harder and harder to fight her off.

"Blood, this shit not right, we can't keep doing this to bro," Paperchase tried to reason with her, but she wasn't trying to hear him.

"What big brother doesn't know won't hurt him. Trust."
Olivia sank her teeth in the side of his neck and began sucking
on it. She then took his hand and slid it inside of her panties.
His fingers parted her rose petals, and he slipped one of his
digits inside of her pink. She was sticky and oozing hot with
her natural juices. The feel of her womanhood made him weak
in the knees. He placed his head back against the wall, rolling
his eyes and licking his lips. He felt her squeezing his piece
while running her delicate hand up and down the length of it.

"You feel that, papi? Huh? You feel that?"

"Y—yeah, mami, I feel that shit," Paperchase replied in a
hushed tone.

"It's so hot, juicy, and tight, just for you, Pa," Olivia
swore, kissing up his neck and then sucking on the soft flesh
below his chin. Clear pre-cum oozed out of his pee-hole and
ran down his shaft. "Tell me you don't want none of this
pussy. You look me in my eyes and tell me you don't want
none of this pussy. If you can do that, I'll stop what I'm doing
right now and leave," she told him between sucking on the soft
flesh below his chin.

"I—I—I don't want none of this p—pussy," Paperchase
managed to tell her with his eyes shut.

As soon as she pulled away from him, his eyes popped
open, and he watched her pick her bra back up. She was about
to put it back on until he pulled her into him. He lifted her up
against the wall, and she wrapped her legs around his waist.
Heavily breathing, they kissed hard and lustfully while he un-
did his jeans hastily. His jeans fell down around his thighs. He
pulled her panties aside and shoved himself deep within her
hidden valley. She threw her head back, fluttering her eyes
and howling in a mixture of pain and bliss. He started fucking
her savagely up against the wall. He knocked over the lamp
on the nightstand in the midst of them getting busy. She

slipped her hands underneath his shirt and clawed at his back. Her acrylic nails broke his skin, and blood seeped from the small wounds. His face balled up in pleasure and pain, and he started fucking her even harder. Her sexual screams bounced off the walls inside of the bedroom. And the banging up against the wall eventually caused a framed portrait to fall.

Ghost & Tranay Adams

20

Chapter 3
Meanwhile

Errrn! The loud buzzer resonated through the federal facility. Metal door after metal door slid open and convicts emerged out of their cells onto the gallery. Among them was Scorpion. He made his way down the tier with a hardened expression on his face. He walked down the stairs and onto the landing. As he walked across the floor, he exchanged daps and "what's up" with the convicts within his organization and mean mug stares with those on the opposing side. He entered the visiting room, handing in his visitor's pass to the officer at the front desk. They swapped a few words before he continued on his way to the person that was visiting him. His head was on a swivel as he scanned every face in attendance. The wave of a pinkish hand caught his attention, and his eyes settled on the man he was looking forward to seeing that evening.

The gentleman waiting at the table for Scorpion went by the name Othman Cromwel. He was a fifty-five-year-old retired homicide detective who now ran his own private investigation firm. He was a heavy-set, clean-shaven man who sported a bald head that shined like a buffed floor. He wore a sports coat over a polo shirt and stonewashed blue jeans. He rose to his feet and extended his hand towards Scorpion.

"Mr. Williams, how have you been?" Othman asked as they shook hands.

"I'm good," Scorpion replied, pulling his pants up at the knees and sitting down at the table.

"Great. You get a chance to check out the game last night? Boy, I tell ya, I had five grand riding on the Cavs, and those fuckers—" Othman was cut short when Scorpion abruptly raised his hand in the middle of him talking.

"Look, bruh, you and I have what you call an employer/ employee relationship, so all that conversing like old college buddies isn't necessary," Scorpion told him with a dead serious look on his face. "I pay you good money for your services, and I'd like to know whether my baby girl is fucking around on me or not."

Something at the back of Scorpion's mind was nagging him about Olivia's loyalty to him. Although she'd sworn up and down that she hadn't been fucking around with anyone else, he couldn't shake the feeling that she wasn't being honest. He tried to tell himself he had a good girl and that she'd never do anything to break his heart, but he'd heard too many niggas behind those walls crying themselves to sleep at night behind their woman getting dick down on the outside. He knew if he didn't find out for sure if his boo was creeping or not that his mind wouldn't allow him to rest, so he decided to enlist Othman to get to the bottom of things and find out exactly what was going on.

Othman looked away, scratching the back of his bald head. He then looked up at Scorpion, who wore a solemn expression as he waited for him to deliver his findings. The heavyset man took a deep breath and leaned closer so only Scorpion could hear what he was about to say.

"Your sweet little angel isn't so innocent," Othman told him in a hushed tone.

The moment the words left his lips, Scorpion felt his heart drop and tumble across the floor. He suddenly felt dizzy and wanted to throw up. The G in him would never allow Othman to see how fucked up he was behind his wifey two-timing him, though.

"What exactly do you mean, bruh? Just come out and say it," Scorpion said with frustration. He was hoping he told him Olivia was calling, texting, or had gone out with some nigga on a date. He was sure they could salvage their relationship and work things out if that was the case. But there was no way they could live happily ever after if she was giving some other nigga what was his. That was something he most definitely couldn't live with. He'd have to off her and whatever clown she was laying up with.

"You know I came in here trying to break the news to you as gently as I possibly can 'cause I'm a nice guy, but if you want the raw uncut truth, I'll give it to ya, buddy," Othman said with a no-nonsense attitude. "That fiancée of yours is getting it long, hard, and fast up the hoo-ha. I'm sorry to have to be the one to tell you, but that's just how it is." He took a deep breath and lay back in his chair.

Scorpion became teary-eyed, clenching and unclenching his jaws while balling his fists. He was angry, hurt, and devastated. The news stung him like the venomous tail of a scorpion. To keep from breaking down and looking soft, Scorpion closed his eyes and ran his hands down his face. He then took a deep breath and scooted his chair up to the table. His heart ached like a mothafucka, but he had to get the question lingering in his head answered.

"A'ight, who is this nigga she's fucking around with?" Scorpion asked.

Othman sat up in his chair and leaned close enough so that only Scorpion could hear him. He told him the name of the person blowing his bitch's back out. His eyes bucked, and his mouth hung open in shock.

***

"Fuck me, brother, fuck me, fuck me! Oh God, yes! Yes!" Olivia hollered loud enough for the Lord and all of his angels in Heaven to hear her. Her eyes were squeezed shut, and her mouth was hanging open. She was high up on the wall with her arms and legs wrapped around Paperchase's waist. He sucked on her neck as he fucked her like a mad man. His back muscles flexed along with his buttocks. He was packing her ass out, running dick in and out of her, with his jeans in a pile around his ankles.

"This my pussy? Huh? This pussy belongs to me?" Paperchase asked with clenched jaws and possessed eyes. He was laying into her like he hated her guts.

"Yes, it's yours, li'l bro, it belongs to you! Only you!" Olivia hollered even louder, making Paperchase fuck her that much harder, grunting.

***

"You cocksucka, I'll kill you!" Scorpion bellowed as he lunged at Othman from the other side of the table. He collided with him, and they slammed into the floor with his hands wrapped around his neck. Straddling him, he squeezed his neck tighter and tighter, with spit hanging from the corner of his mouth. "I'll kill you! I'll fucking kill you, you mothafucka!"

"Ack, ack, ack, gag, gag, ack!" Othman turned beet red, and veins bulged over his forehead. His eyes widened, and he became teary. He tried his hardest to pry Scorpion's hands from around his neck, but his adrenaline added to his strength, made that impossible.

"You're lying. You're fucking lying!" Scorpion shouted with spit jumping off his lips and his eyes twinkling with tears.

All of the inmates and visitors in the room were looking at them in shock.

Othman looked like he was about to lose consciousness from lack of oxygen. He stopped trying to fight Scorpion off and lay there, letting him choke him.

"Die, die, you fucking asshole!" Scorpion hollered, and his spit clung to Othman's face.

***

The hot shower water began to fog the bathroom mirror while Paperchase studied his reflection. Hunched over the sink, he looked at himself like he didn't know who he was, having betrayed his brother by sleeping with Olivia. He'd tried a million times, but he couldn't stop fucking her. It was like he was a dope fiend, and she was the heroine. He was addicted to her.

"Damn, a nigga never thought he'd end up pussy whipped, but here I am." Paperchase shook his head sadly. He was ashamed. He could tell himself once again that this would be the last time he laid up with Olivia, but deep down inside, he knew he'd be lying to himself. He honestly didn't know what he was going to do if his brother was released from prison. "Fuck it. I'll just cross that bridge with bro once I come to it."

"Boy, who are you talking to?" Olivia asked as she stepped behind him naked and wrapped her arms around him. She placed the side of her face against his and looked at their reflections in the mirror. She started kissing on the side of his face and alongside his neck.

"No one—just thinking aloud." Paperchase flashed a weak smile and kissed her over his shoulder.

"Come on. I'ma need you to wash my back." Olivia smiled happily as she led him over to the glass enclosure by his hand.

***

Othman sat up on the floor with teary eyes coughing and rubbing his aching neck. A corrections officer was on either side of him, making sure he was okay.

"I'll be—I'll be fine," Othman nodded as he assured them.

"You liar, you fucking piece of shit!" Scorpion screamed over and over again as he was being hauled away by three corrections officers, with his wrists cuffed behind his back. He struggled against their stronghold, twisting, turning, and kicking his legs wildly. He was acting a goddamn fool inside of that visitors' room and didn't show any signs of slowing down.

The corrections officers assisted Othman back upon his feet. He stood between them, rubbing his neck and looking at Scorpion being drugged away.

"Paperchase would never do that to me, you lying bastard!" Scorpion screamed again. "You fucked with the wrong one. Now you'll pay! You're a dead man! You hear me? You're a dead man!"

Chapter 4

Once Paperchase and Olivia had showered, one thing led to another and they wound up getting busy again. Paperchase had broken her off real proper like. He had that ass laid on her back breathing funny like a gunshot victim. Once she recovered, she dipped off to the kitchen to retrieve a little something that was going to spice things up. Olivia came out of the kitchen with a bottle of chocolate syrup in her left hand. With her right hand she kept her juices flowing by rubbing her pussy mound in a circular motion. Her essence seeped out of her and traveled down her thick thighs all the way to her slender ankles. She stepped into the doorway and cleared her throat sexily.

Paperchase sat up in the bed with his chest muscles jumping as if he'd just got down from an intense workout. He was puffing on a Dutch Master that was stuffed with some of the best purple buds flowing through New York. "Nah, shorty, I ain't fuckin' with you, I gotta get in traffic. I done already lost a couple hunnit laying up with yo' ass." He took five more puffs from his blunt and stubbed it out. Then he started to ease out of the bed.

Olivia dropped the chocolate syrup and dove on top of him to stop his leaving. Her small hand wrapped right around his thick dick that seemed to go on forever and a day. She squeezed it and rubbed his head all over her succulent lips. In the blink of an eye, she was sucking him like a top notch porn star. "Nigga, you ain't going nowhere until I'm done riding this big-ass dick."

Paperchase closed his eyes and groaned. "Damn, Liv, stall a nigga out for a minute."

"Ain't!" She turned her face to the side and slurped him louder and louder already knowing that the sound effects drove him out of his mind. She slipped her right hand under

27

her stomach and diddled her clitoris. She could already imagine his dick going back inside of her, filling her up as only he had been able to. Lord knows that she loved Scorpion, and before she'd seen Paperchase naked she swore up and down that nobody was built like her man, but then she caught sight of his little brother and all bets were off. Ever since he'd hit regions inside of her that she never even knew existed, all she could think about was locking him down indefinitely. There was no way that any other bitch was about to get their hands on Paperchase - not without her draining him first.

Paperchase watched her head dance up and down in his lap. She added so much spit that it dripped off of his balls, and then came her tongue, cleaning up the mess that she made. He could smell her breath radiating off of his piece. "Fuck, Olivia, bitch, you wiling."

She slid up his body and reached between them, taking a hold of his dick that was throbbing up against her ass crack. She took it and slid down on it, shivering as inch after inch filled her. "Mmm, just let me get this last nut, baby brother. Please, that's all sis wants is to cum on her little brother's dick one more time and den you can go." She moaned louder and arched her back, riding him passionately. "Un! Un! Unhhhh, fuck, baby bruh! Fuck yo' sister pussy!"

Paperchase grabbed a hold of her ass and squeezed it tightly as she rode him. He became forceful, slamming her down on him, making sure that she was taking all of the dick every time. She dug her nails into his shoulder blades and screamed with white cum sudsing up all around his stalk.

Paperchase flipped her over and forced her knees into her under arms. He took his huge dick and stuffed it back into her. "Bitch, you just can't get enough, can you? You just gotta have this dick, don't you? Huh, bitch? Huh? Huh? Huh?" he growled, rolling his back and slamming into her pussy. "You know we ain't right!"

"Uhhhhh!" She sat up and bit into his neck, then she fell to her back. "Fuck yo' sister! Fuck me! Fuck me harder, Paperchase! Uhhh, shit, baby. I love this dick! I love it!" She came and started to shake again.

Paperchase started to fuck her so hard that all he could do was clench his teeth and zoom into how pretty her light brown, hard nipples stood out from her mounds, and the way her globes danced for him. She looked so fine moaning with her thick lips. When her tongue traced her entire mouth and she bucked, he envisioned his brother's angry face and came hollering into the crux of her neck.

Olivia smiled, digging her nails into his back. "Nut in me, baby brother. Nut in this pussy, it's yours! I swear it's all yours!"

Paperchase came and came again and then fell on top of her with his piece twitching inside of her like crazy. He couldn't help but to see Scorpion's angry face with a set of prison bars in front of them. Suddenly remorse for screwing his brother's woman came over him like a dark cloud. He pulled out of her pussy and came to his knees.

Olivia rubbed her slit and sucked her fingers. She loved their taste. There was something about it that drove her crazy. She looked up to Paperchase and noticed a sick expression written across his handsome face. She furrowed her eyebrows. "What's the matter?"

Chapter 5

Paperchase walked into the bathroom and turned on the shower. "Yo, on some real shit, that was our last time getting down. I can't keep fuckin' over my brother like this, shorty. That's bitch nigga shit, and ain't shit bitch about me." He climbed into the tub and pulled the shower curtain closed

Olivia ran her fingers through her hair. She got out of the bed and came into the bathroom with his semen leaking out of her. "Look, Maurice, I know every time we get down you start to have remorse and all of that, and I understand where you are coming from, but your brother ain't coming home for a really long-ass time. Would you rather me fuck' off wit' some other nigga instead? I mean, what am I to do?"

"Bitch, I don't know, but I like to go visit my nigga and all of that good shit, but it's getting to the point that I can't even look blood in the eyes. That shit weak. That's my brother."

"I know who he is, but who am I to you then?" She honestly wanted to know how he saw her.

'Paperchase started to wash his long dick with the body wash and her loofah. "You're my brother's bitch, plain and simple. Fuck you thought you was?"

Olivia winced in emotional pain. She swallowed and took a step back to gather herself. "Yo, so that's it?"

The water ran into Paperchase's face. "That's it. I mean, I guess since blood talking about tying the knot wit'chu that'll make you my sister, but beyond all that, that's it."

Olivia balled her fist for a moment. She had to calm down. She could smell the mixture of the body wash and their sex on him. She ripped the shower curtain back just as he was scrubbing his balls. "Yo, so you mean to tell me that you ain't feeling nothing for me?"

Paperchase was silent for a moment. He knew that he had to choose his words carefully. There was no way that he could admit that he was developing strong feelings for his brother's woman. That was out of the question because he already knew that they had no future together. "Yo, from here on out, all I'ma see you as is my sister. I ain't fuckin' wit'chu on no sexual level no more. We need to come together and get bro up out of there."

"Nigga, that ain't what I asked yo' black ass. Do you have any feelings for me whatsoever?" Olivia asked this, walking up on him so close that water was popping on to her naked body from off of his.

"Nah, shorty, ain't no future in that shit, so why entertain that thought?" He laughed and turned the water off. He grabbed a towel and wrapped it around his lower region. He kissed her on the cheek. "It's best that you don't develop none of that shit for me either because ain't shit moving, that's on gang." He walked past her.

She mugged the back of his head for a long time while she stood in one place, watching him get dressed. She slowly walked into the bedroom. "You know what, Maurice? I don't know what it is you're trying to pull on me, but I know better. I'm a few years older than you. I can tell when a nigga feeling somethin' for a bitch and I'm definitely in ya chest plate. You just holding back because yo' punk ass is feeling guilty. Nigga, you ain't gotta be with me, but at least have enough acorns to admit that you feel something for me. Don't have me feeling like I'm just another random bitch you was fuckin' out of convenience."

"Nah, shorty, it wasn't out of convenience. It was more like a nigga was forced to tap that ass."

"Forced! Are you kidding me?"

"Nah, I mean just thank about it. Bitch, how many times did you flash a nigga? How many times you kissed all over me on some other shit? Then thank about how we first started to fuckin'. You see what I'm sayin'? That was all you. But it's on me to end this shit, and that's what I'm doing. It's over - tonight." He slipped his light Chanel jacket over his shoulders and zipped it up. Then he tucked both .9 millimeters into his waistband. He glanced over at her and grinned. "Why you looking all mad and shit?"

She shook her head. "No reason, bruh, it's all good. I am going to ask you to leave right now though." She grabbed her robe and slipped it over her frame, neglecting to tie the sash, thereby keeping her nakedness on display. She walked to the front door and opened it for him.

Paperchase stepped up to it and looked her up and down. She was fine - too damn fine, he had to admit - but he had to stop fucking her. She didn't belong to him. She was Scorpion's. "Yo, no hard feelings, Liv, you know I got mad love for you, right?"

"Good night, Maurice. I pray you make it home safely. The streets are crazy right now."

He leaned in to kiss her cheek but she stepped back. "That's what we on now?"

"Good night, li'l brother. I'm tired."

Paperchase laughed. "Damn, that's cold. I guess I'll fuck wit' you tomorrow then."

"Nah. blood, why don't you social distance for a few days. I'll reach out when I'm ready to see ya stupid face again." She slammed the door in his face and locked it. "Fuck nigga. I got his ass though. Wanna jump up and down inside of me and then make me feel like a fool for the fuckin' feelings I developed? Yeah, a'ight, Paperchase. I got yo' ass real good."

***

Ramone could feel his heart pounding harder and harder inside of his chest as he looked across the street and saw Paperchase coming out of Olivia's house and jumping into his 2022 black-on-black Escalade that he had sitting up on thirty-inch gold Davens. As soon as Paperchase hopped into the truck, Ramone ran out into the middle of the street hopped up off cocaine, busting.

Bocka! Bocka! Bocka! Bocka!

His bullets ate up the side of Paperchase's truck, shattering the windows and causing the truck to shake from side to side. Paperchase ducked all the way down and took his Glizzies off his waist. He cursed under his breath. Olivia heard the gunshots and stupidly ran to the window to see who it was that was shooting on her block. When she saw the shooting pair of Boobie and Durty step out from behind the blue Chevy Caprice Classic that they had been hiding behind, she dropped to the carpet and whispered Paperchase's name out loud.

Paperchase pushed open the passenger's door and rolled out onto the sidewalk. He hurried back to his truck and waited for a cease in their firing before he stood tall and began to yak from over the top of the roof of the Cadillac. "Pussy-ass niggas!"

Blocka! Blocka! Blocka! Blocka!

Ramone stumbled backward, finger fucking his trigger. The bump stock made bullets fly rapidly, inaccurate. His slugs crashed into the neighbor's house and knocked their television off of the wall. Another round of his slugs shattered their fish tank. He took off running down the street, stopping every now and then to turn around and bust back at Paperchase.

Paperchase saw him take off and took it upon himself to aim and fire. A slug caught Ramone in his right shoulder and knocked him to the ground. He hollered at the top of his lungs. Paperchase took off running toward him absentmindedly, forgetting about Boobie and Durty. He didn't make it more than ten steps before they tried to gun him down. Out of instinct, Paperchase ducked and fired back to back. Boobie thought that Paperchase fell because he had been hit so he ran out into the middle of the street to finish him. Paperchase aimed and squeezed his trigger three times, catching Boobie twice through the neck. His Adam's apple flew on to the curb. Boobie twisted and slammed his head against the side of a parked car before he began to twitch violently. Durty hollered and ran into the street, squeezing his gun to the sound of a bunch of clicking already having run out of bullets. Olivia hawked him from the porch with her .380 six times, running toward him. She ran past Paperchase and finished Durty. With her gun smoking, she hurried over to Paperchase's side and helped him to his feet. "Nigga, you good?"

Paperchase dusted himself off, and looked down the block just as Ramone disappeared around the block. He turned his sights to her and looked her up and down, jerking away from her. "Yo, don't think you saved my life or some shit like that. I was about to drill that nigga too. Trust that."

Olivia scoffed and took a step back so that she could see him more clearly. "Yo, that's what the fuck you on, homeboy? Especially after I just saved ya ass from being placed on the front of niggas' shirts in the hood?"

Paperchase mugged her and snatched her up to him. "Liv, I ain't playing wit'cho ass. Don't go telling this story like I'm a bitch or something. I would've caught that nigga before he caught me. You stepped in because you wanted to. I ain't need you to do shit."

Olivia pushed him off of her. "The fuck off of me. Yo, you tripping. We gotta get up off of the block before the Jakes come through this bitch locking ma'fuckas up and all of that. I can't believe you." She started to walk off with her eyes still planted on the two dead bodies before them.

Paperchase grabbed a hold of her wrist and pulled her to him. "I ain't playing though. Keep ya fuckin' mouth closed about this shit right here, and we good."

She sucked her teeth and nodded her head. "Yeah, a'ight, bruh, this shit goes with us to the grave. She snatched her wrist out of his grasp, took two steps, and stopped. "No matter what the fuck you say though, you're welcome." She rolled her eyes and jogged into the house.

Police car sirens wailed loudly in the distance as Paperchase turned around and made his way back to the masked shooters he and Olivia had slumped. He tucked his banger at the small of his back and kneeled down to the first shooter. He pulled off his ski mask and was shocked to see who it was. That nigga Boobie! He had to be sure his mind wasn't playing tricks on him so he checked the unique tattoos Boobie was known to sport.

If this is Boobie, then who the fuck is Blood Liv laid down? Paperchase wondered as he looked at the other masked shooter. He pulled the dead man's mask up above his brows, revealing his identity. It was that nigga Durty.

"Now why in the hell would two of the homies and a white boy be tryna flatline a nigga?" Papechase said under his breath as he pulled the mask back over Durty's face. He looked around at all of the carnage and sighed. Every time he wanted to find it within himself to get rid of Olivia, she always had a way of pulling him back. With the current events that had recently taken place, he found himself smitten and seriously weak for her in a way that made him sick on the stomach.

I've gotta push shorty to the back of my mind for the time being. Right now I gotta holla at my nigga. Shit just got real.

Paperchase hit up Jabari as he made his way toward his Escalade truck. He answered on the third ring.

"Yo, son, you ain't gon' believe what the fuck just happened to the kid." Paperchase told him. "Nah, I'm not choppin' it up on this jack. We've gotta link up."

Paperchase gave Jabari the location of a spot outside of the city's limits that they were both familiar with. When Jabari pressed him again about what he was calling the meeting for, he told him to be there and hung up.

Jabari wasn't quite sure what to think. A million thoughts raced through his mind, and a million scenarios, all of which ended up with his black ass being dead. He figured it was better to be safe than sorry so he strapped on a bulletproof vest and loaded up two automatic pistols. He even got a special-customized vehicle for that particular night: a bulletproof black Mercedes Sprinter van. For all he knew, Paperchase found out he was the one who'd orchestrated the hit on him, and he was walking into an ambush.

Chapter 6

Paperchase showed up an hour early at the meet-up spot just to be on the safe side. He parked his Escalade diagonally at the back of the old Shell gas station that had been closed for quite some time. The establishment's windows and all of its entrances and exits had been boarded up, and they were all covered in colorful graffiti. There was loose trash scattered on the ground, and weeds had grown out of the cracks in the cement.

A rat ran past Paperchase's foot, but he didn't pay it any mind. He was busy pacing the ground, puffing on a Newport and trying to figure out who wanted him dead. One hand held his cigarette while the other lingered near the banger in his waistband. Homie was jumpy! With every sound he was drawing down to blow a nigga's face off.

Paperchase dropped what must have been his tenth cigarette and mashed it out into the ground. He was about to withdraw another square from his carton of smokes when he was suddenly bathed in the headlights of an oncoming van.

"Blood, who the fuck is this?" Paperchase said under his breath, straining his eyes to see who was in the suspicious vehicle. His street nigga sense, much like a Spider sense, kicked in. He spat the Newport to the ground and reached for his waistband. The vehicle stopped before him and its headlights died. He was able to identify it then: a black Mercedes-Benz Sprinter.

Paperchase didn't know anyone pushing a Mercedes-Benz, so he figured it was loaded with shooters. Upping his piece, he went to open fire until a pair of hands came out of the driver's window, letting him know they weren't armed.

"Relax, my nigga, it's just me: Jabari!" Jabari announced.

Paperchase sighed with relief and tucked his tool in his waistband. The driver's door of the Sprinter swung open and Jabari hopped out. He slammed the door behind him, scanned the area for any signs of a threat, and then made his way over to his right-hand man. He shook up with Paperchase and gave him a thug hug.

"What up, my G? What chu call me out here for?" Jabari asked, playing ignorant to the fact.

How in the fuck did li'l bruh and them miss this nigga, man? Goddamn! On gang, muthafuckas can't do nothing right.

"Three niggas tried to take me out tonight, Slime."

Jabari looked at him like he was bullshitting. "Get the fuck outta here, B."

"Real spit."

"You got any idea who it may be?"

"Nah. But it's gotta be gang."

"What? Fuck makes you think that?"

"Well, one of 'em was a white nigga, and two of 'em were of Woo."

Jabari frowned and folded his arms across his chest. His scandalous ass deserved a nominee for his performance. He was just that damn convincing!

"Yo, son, you been my nigga forever and a day." Jabari gripped his shoulder, holding his gaze. "Word to everything I love and then some, you tell me who these fools are, and we'll go smoke 'em right now."

Feeling his cell phone vibrating inside his pocket, Jabari pulled it out and held up a finger. "Li'l Bruh" was on the display. It was Ramone hitting him up. Jabari pressed "ignore" and stuck his cellular back inside his pocket. "Go head, bro."

"Who was that?"

He shook his head and said, "This li'l skeeza I be fuckin' with. Never mind her though. I wanna know who these niggas are that got at my brother?"

"It was Boobie and Durty, but chu ain't gotta worry about them bitch-ass niggas though."

"Why's that?"

"'Cause me and Liv laid them goofies down."

"Word?"

Paperchase nodded. "The white boy that was with 'em got away, but I swear 'fore God if I ever catch up with him, I'ma put his face in the dirt. Ya heard?" Paperchase scowled and balled his fists at his sides.

"Boobie and Durty are two of our best shooters," Jabari told him. "Bro used them for a lotta wet work."

"Bro? Who we talkin' 'bout, son?" Paperchase narrowed his eyes and looked at him sideways. Jabari communicated to him who he was talking about through his eyes. "My brother? Scorpion? Hell naw, Slime. He wouldn't! I'm his blood." Jabari looked at him like *Nigga, you know how Scorpion rolls.*

At that moment, Paperchase's mind flashed back to what his brother had said about bodying any nigga he found out was fucking Olivia. He recalled him saying he didn't care who it was, they were dead! From the look in his eyes, he could tell that he was as serious as a positive test result for herpes. Paperchase thought about what Jabari had said for a minute. No matter how he looked at it, he didn't see his brother sending Boobie and Durty at him.

"Nah. If big bro was to send some steppas to knock me down, he wouldn't use anyone from Woo."

"You sure about that?"

"You fuckin' right I am. That's my brother. I know his get down," Paperchase told him. "He wouldn't use any of our hittas 'cause he wouldn't want the job being traced back to him.

My nigga smarter than that. Blood would have sent some outta town killas to blow my ass off the map."

Jabari massaged his chin as he thought about it. He nodded, thinking that Paperchase had a good point. He always was the smarter one out of the two of them. "Well, if it ain't the big homie, then who?"

"I don't know, my nigga, but when I find out, you'll be the first to know." Paperchase outstretched his hand.

"And when you hit me up, that's on Woo and 'em grave, we choppin' niggas heads off." Jabari shook up with him and gave him another thug hug. "Straight like that."

"Straight like that. Love, fool."

"Love, my nigga."

Jabari broke their embrace, hopped back inside the Mercedes-Benz Sprinter van, and cranked it up. He spent the next couple of minutes acting like he was doing something until Paperchase hopped in his whip and drove off. As soon as he was out of sight, Jabari honked his horn and motioned someone over from the driver's window. The shadows stirred. Then two masked demons with assault rifles came running from out of the darkness. Their shadows cast on the side of the old gas station.

The masked men hopped into the Sprinter van and Jabari closed the door. As soon as he drove away, the demons pulled off their ski mask and wiped their sweaty forehead. Jabari had dropped his demons Spank and Jibbs off on the opposite side of the gas station. He then drove around to the other side where Paperchase was waiting for him. Spanks and Jibbs were to blow Paperchase away along with anyone else that posed a threat.

Although Jabari didn't want to see his childhood friend gunned down in cold blood, he was willing to give the kill signal to his steppas if his life was in danger. Thankfully, he hadn't been ambushed, and he was able to walk away from the meeting without blood on his hands. He'd much rather be far away from the kill zone when his best friend was crushed for fear of seeing it happen haunting him for the rest of his days.

"Yo, Jabari, you shoulda let us stank homie," Jibbs said before lighting up his half of blunt. He took a couple of pulls of it and passed it to Spank, who indulged in it.

"Hell yeah, Blood. We coulda smoked him and got this shit over with," Spank chimed in, holding smoke in his lungs. Clouds of smoke had the back of the Mercedes Sprinter van looking like a sauna.

As soon as Jabari stopped at a red traffic light, he shot a death stare over his shoulder at Spank and Jibbs. They shut the fuck up real quick, knowing how he gave it up. Jabari focused his attention back on the streets, pulling through the intersection once the light had turned green. He turned the volume up on Benny the Butcher's "Burden of Proof" to drown out the silence in the van.

Jabari didn't give a mad-ass fuck about that shit Spank and Jibbs were popping. Paperchase had been his dawg for as long as he could remember. The nigga was practically his blood brother. It wasn't like he was some regular old street nigga. Had he been, he would have been knocked him down, without question, but that wasn't the case. The situation was delicate, so he'd have to handle it with care because without a doubt, he'd have to live with knowing he'd betrayed his right-hand man for a come on.

Jabari drove along with tears cascading down his cheeks, thinking of all the shit he and Paperchase had been through. It broke his heart knowing he had to lay his man down to ensure his passage into dope game royalty. Jabari wiped his face, sniffled, and pulled his nose. Spank and Jibbs exchanged glances, witnessing him shed tears. If they didn't know then, they knew now that even gangstas cry.

***

Three hours later, Olivia sat on the edge of the hotel room's bed, reading a novel by Jelissa Shante called *Love Me Even When It Hurts*, one her favorite novels by that author. She found a way to completely block Paperchase out, even as he sat at the night table just a few feet away from her counting thirty thousand dollars in cash. She found herself so consumed with what she was reading that it didn't register that he was still there until he nudged her on the arm.

"Yo, Liv, what you reading?" He tied a rubber band around a ten thousand dollar knot and proceeded to do the same thing with the rest of the money that was present.

"I'm sitting here trying to read, but clearly you ain't about to let that happen, so how may I help you, Paperchase?" Sue sat down on her tablet and looked at him, disinterested.

"Look, I ain't mean to come at you all reckless and shit earlier. On some real nigga shit though, you held me down against the opp and I ain't got nothing but love for you for doing so. I know plenty niggas that wouldn't have been able to hold their own in that situation, or they never would have showed up to begin with. The fact that you came through says a lot about you."

Olivia side-eyed him. 'Say what?" She turned to face him, sitting Indian style.

"Yo, stop playing, you heard what I just said. Huh, here go a little bit of nothing as a token of my appreciation." He held a ten thousand dollar bundle out for her to receive.

She pushed his hand away, "I don't need ya money boss, I got my own." She went back to reading her tablet for a while, then she slammed it down. "Yo, what I don't understand is how you can keep saying that you got love for me, but yo' ass is afraid to admit that you ACTUALLY love me. I don't get it. You're acting like there are a whole bunch of people here to witness how you're feeling. So why you can't admit it?"

Paperchase dropped the money in her lap and waved her off. "Shorty, the last thing I'm trying to do right now is get all emotional and shit. I said what I said, so let's leave that shit right there."

She shook her head and hopped up stepping into his face. "Nah, Paperchase, you don't get to make that decision. I think with me saving yo' life and all of that right there that I deserve your truth, so be honest, do you love me?"

Paperchase dropped his head. "Damn, Liv, who gives a fuck if I do or not?"

"Nigga, I do, so what's to it?" She tilted his chin downward so that he was looking directly in her eyes. "Holla at'cha girl."

Paperchase removed her hand and nodded. "Yeah, I do. I'm feeling you way more than I should. Scorpion should get out and drop me on sight. This shit is weak as a bitch."

Olivia squealed, "No he shouldn't." She wrapped her arms around his neck, then kissed him on the lips over and over again. "Yo, I swear I love you too. I knew I wasn't going crazy and I wanna kick ya ass for making me feel like I am. Damn, boy." She laid her head on his chest. "I already know we done fucked up, and it ain't gon' make it no better carrying yo' seed and all." She looked up at him, took two steps back, and rested her hand over her stomach.

"My seed? What you talking about, Liv?"

She stroked the sides of his face. "I'm pregnant, and I ain't never been happier."

Paperchase stood her up so that she was facing him. He looked her directly in the eyes. "Yo, what are you saying? Cuz you're freaking me the hell out right now."

"I'm sayin' you and I are going to be parents. Isn't that just the best thing you've ever heard?" She hugged herself and smiled brightly.

Paperchase took a step back and looked her over. He placed his right hand to her stomach and gazed into her eyes again. "Yo, you shitting me. Tell me you yanking my chain right now."

Olivia's smile turned into a frown, "Why the hell would I be doing that? We're pregnant, and that's just what it is. Now, what are you going to do?"

Chapter 7

Jabari paced back and forth inside of the damp basement with sweat sliding down the sides of his face. He clenched his fists over and over again and took one deep breath after the next. "Yo, so tell me again how the fuck one nigga managed to blow down the three of y'all? This shit is not making sense to me."

Ramone sat on a blue milk crate while one of the hood bitches out of the Red Hook Housing Projects removed his bullet, sterilized, and sewed him back up to perfection. Jabari had waited for her to leave before he began his questioning again. There were large spiders crawling all over the brick walls. Small mice ran along the edges of the concrete screeching loudly. Only two days prior Jabari and three of his Woo members had cut up and discarded the bodies of two Opps. The basement was known to them as their Murder Quarters.

"Yo, I don't know how it happened. One moment we were on that nigga's ass ready to drill him, and the next he was bucking at us with accuracy. I caught one to the shoulder and ducked around the corner. When I did, Boobie and Durty were still alive. Seeing this shit on the news blew my top off too. Shit, I thought they were still behind me, to be honest with you."

Jabari punched his hand as hard as he could. "Damn, man, that nigga always had the luck of the Irish. I don't feel like dealing with Sanka's clown ass. I'm ready to get this Rebirth and get to it. Every second this nigga got breath inside of his body is another second that I ain't able to do what the fuck I need to do to take over this muthafucka. You three niggas had a simple-ass task and y'all couldn't even do that. I ain't understanding this shit for nothing. Fuck if I ever am."

Ramone dropped his head. The three Percocets were just starting to take effect. His body suddenly felt calm and relaxed. "I tried to, kid, word to Jehovah, I did. This was really my first drill session and I learned a lot. Who would have ever thought that Paperchase would be clapping back like that against three gunners? That shit says a lot right there."

"That doesn't say shit. All it says is that I sent three bitch-ass niggas to do a man's job. If I was there, I would have slumped his bitch-ass with no problem. Y'all niggas just clowns."

"I ain't no clown, B. I'm Woo, nigga. I ain't win this gunfight. You couldn't have won every one of yours either. I ain't buying that shit if you say that you did either."

"Bitch, I don't play with these sticks. If I want yo' ass dead, yo' pussy ass is gone. I don't miss. I'm a legend in these streets. Niggas know what Jabari do. That's why they fear the god. That fool Paperchase is supposed to be chalked already. But it's good though, 'cause next time I'ma handle it, or at least get a shooter that really can. Incompetent-ass niggas."

Ramone stood up. He winced from the severe shoulder pain. He mugged Jabari. "Yo, I know you feeling a way and all of that, but I ain't about to sit here and let you keep shooting slugs at me like I'm pussy or somethin'. That shit ain't about to keep happening."

Jabari side-eyed him, and the images of a stretched out Jayshawn caused an evil smile to spread across his lips. "Yeah, you're right, li'l bruh, that's my bad. I ain't mean nothing by it. You're all good. I'm sure that you did the best that you could do, and that's all that matters." He leaned into him and gave him a half hug.

"I tried, B. You should know that I respect you way too much to not have."

48

"I know you did, and it's all good." He finished his half of a hug and stepped back. "Yo, after all of that shit, I need you to lay low for at least a week. Just chill with yo' peoples, and I'll touch bases with you when this shit dies down. Go find ya moms. I know that's at the top of yo' priority list. That's important."

Ramone wanted to ask him how he knew, but he decided against it. He just understood that Jabari was connected to the streets, and that very few things got past him. So instead of disputing his claims he nodded and walked out of the basement, honestly thankful to be alive.

***

Ramone found Martha in a well-known heroin house, laid out flat on the floor with her dress pulled up to her dirty bra. Her hair had roaches crawling inside and all over it, and there were ants walking all over the ham sandwich that she had beside her. Ramone bent down to his knees and pulled her up to him.

Martha slowly opened her eyes. Her tongue was so dry that it hurt when it moved around inside of her mouth. Her head, body, and vagina were pounding so bad that she groaned in agony. "I don't wanna do anything else. Y'all are hurting me. Let me go!" She yanked away from her son, not knowing that it was him, but instead surmising that it was another addict trying to take sexual advantage of her body.

"Yo, Moms, chill, it's me, Ramone." He guided her pretty face with his hand to make her face him.

It took a second for Martha's eyes to focus on Ramone. When she was finally able to identify her son, her eyes welled up with tears. "I'm sorry, baby. It's all my fault. If I would have been a better mother to y'all, this would have never happened."

Ramone was confused. "Mama, what are you talking about?" He pulled her dress down so that it covered her decently.

"The devil did that to him because he was my son. It wasn't his fault. I love y'all so much. I just don't know what to do."

Ramone frowned and helped her to come to a standstill after ten minutes of getting her to her feet. He brushed her curly hair out of her face. "What are you talking about, Queen? You're not making any sense right now."

Martha was dope sick and her body began to ache all over. She grabbed a hold of her ribs with her arms in a hugging fashion. "I'm not high, baby, I need a fix. Can you get Mama one? Please? I promise I'll pay you back, li'l daddy." She kissed his cheek. She smelled like musk and two week old unwashed coochie.

All around there were dope addicts crawling on the floor. The majority of them groaned in pain, or moaned in ecstasy. Some argued over the last fix, while others picked bugs off of their unwashed bodies. The place smelled like a sewer system after it rained in New York City along with meth smoke, and that of tobacco.

"Yo, I ain't giving you no ends to keep killing yourself. Come on, we leaving this joint right now."

Martha slumped to the floor. "Ain't!"

Ramone tried his best to pick her back up with her fighting against him. "Ma, come on, don't do this right here. I gotta get you home. Please, I'm begging you."

"I need a fix, Ramone! He killed your brother! They killed my oldest baby. I can't deal with this right now. Please just give me some money so I can cope. I can't take this shit anymore."

"Jayshawn? What do you mean he killed Jayshawn? Who did that?"

Martha cried her eyes out louder and louder. "It's all my fault! I didn't mean to not pay. They said they were going to hurt one of y'all and they did it. They should have taken me. Not my babies. I hate this world!" she screamed.

Ramone dropped to his knees. "They killed Jayshawn? But who? Who killed my brother?"

He found himself crumbling and curling into a ball, crying his eyes out at the imaginings of such a thing. While he broke down, Martha slowly eased away from him, then climbed out of the window, running full speed down the block, occasionally looking over her shoulder as if she were being chased by a crazed serial killer.

Chapter 8

The mess hall was alive with convicts moving down the line, getting the day's slop dumped on their tray. The lunch tables were separated by races: the Blacks, Whites, Latinos, Asians, Pacific Islanders, and Native Americans. The cons only had so much time to eat, so there was little talking.

Scorpion sat at the table claimed by the Woo. He wasn't any different from the rest of the fools on lock. He followed the ritual of eating, drinking and watching everything around him. He locked eyes with Hoffa who was making his way across the floor alongside his hittas. The head of the Muslims communicated to him through eye contact that he was going to have that information he'd earned that day, then he tapped his fist against his chest, letting him know his word was bond. Scorpion nodded understandingly and returned the gesture.

Hoffa sat at the lunch table with his hittas. They prayed over their food and prepared to eat. Scorpion shook his carton of milk up and opened it. He was about to take a drink when a weird feeling came over him. Frowning, he set the milk carton down and looked around him. He saw the shot caller for the Nigerians and a few of his steppas mean mugging Hoffa and his savages, but they didn't seem bothered at all. In fact, one of Hoffa's men, while keeping an eye on the Nigerians' table, whispered something to him. Hoffa, who had just tucked a napkin inside the collar of his shirt, looked up at the Nigerian shot caller, Akachukwu, which meant The Hand of God. He was a 5'7" man of medium build. He was as black as nine o'clock at night with a receding hairline, beaded hair, and a buck-fifty scar that stretched from his forehead, over his nose, and disappeared underneath his chin.

Akachukwu balled his fist, stuck out his thumb, and pretended to cut his throat. This let Hoffa know he was a dead man. When Hoffa's chief hitta peeped the threat, he made to get up from the table, but Hoffa stretched his arm across his chest, keeping him seated.

"Relax, brother, you'll get your chance to leave that cretin lying belly up, in time. For now, we'll play things cool, make our friends think everything is good, and then when they least expect it, we strike - like a Black Mamba, the most poisonous of snakes." Hoffa told him this while keeping his eyes on Akachukwu. His chief enforcer nodded understandingly, adjusted himself in his seat and went back to eating.

Akachukwu kept a close eye on Hoffa as he took a bite of his food. After the first bite came another, then another, and then another. Suddenly, Hoffa's eyes bulged like they were about to pop out of their sockets. He gagged, coughed, spat food, and grabbed his neck. His throat swelled up, making it difficult for him to breathe. He looked at Akachukwu accusingly, who was smiling evilly at him. Right then, Hoffa's eyes rolled to their whites and he fell off the bench dead. As his fellow Muslims crowded around him to see what had occurred, the Nigerian shot caller gave a nod of acknowledgement to the convict in the kitchen that had served Hoffa what was his last meal, which was poisoned by cashews. Hoffa had a nut allergy; that was what killed him.

The corrections officers rushed in, backing the Muslims hittas away from Hoffa. They looked on helplessly, watching their buck-eyed fearless leader lying lifelessly.

"Allah, don't let this be happenin'! Please, don't let this be happenin'!" Scorpion looked up at The Almighty after seeing Hoffa fall to his death.

***

Scorpion had gotten word that Hoffa was indeed dead. It hurt twice as much since he not only lost a friend, but the information he needed to guarantee his release from prison as well. Immediately, the Nigerians and the Muslims went at it and the facility was placed on lockdown. The aftermath left casualties and injuries on both sides. Akachukwu was one among them. Niggas turned him into a pincushion, they put so many holes in him. He was recovering from the savage attack in the infirmary - but not for long, if Scorpion had it his way.

Scorpion sat on the edge of his prison bed with his face in his hands. It was two-thirty in the morning and another night where he'd found it nearly impossible to get so much as an hour of sleep without images of Paperchase and Olivia screwing behind his back. As much as he didn't want to believe it, the dreams of their infidelity never ceased to plague him. He shook his head and started to pace back and forth inside of the room, mumbling to himself.

Booker, his one hundred and thirty pound cellmate, woke up and squinted his eyes down at Scorpion. The constant sounds of Scorpion's bare feet thumping on the floor were enough to awake him. "Yo Blood, what the fuck are you doing?"

Scorpion wanted to ignore him. He wiped the tear from his cheek and waved him off. "Nigga, take ya ass back to sleep. I'm trying to figure some shit out right now." He wiped his eyes out again.

Booker sat up. "Yo, nigga, I been bunked wit' ya ass for damn near eight months now, B. I know when shit ain't kosher wit' you. Dunn, what the bidness is? Fuck the dumb shit, word up."

"Nah, nigga, it ain't shit. I'm just going through one for a minute. Real life shit, that's all." Scorpion sat on the metal toilet in the back of the cell and hung his head.

"Yeah, well nigga, every time you go to sleep, you calling out ya dame's name, asking her how could she. I ain't a rocket scientist; I'm a pill hea. But I still know you gotta be stressing over a bitch. Watch out, nigga, I gotta piss like a race horse." He hopped out of the top bunk. The boisterous sounds of his feet hitting the cement resonated throughout the six by nine feet cell. He was dark-skinned with a head so bald and shiny you could see your reflection in it.

Scorpion stood up and walked to the bars. He kept his back turned so that Booker could have an ample amount of privacy. "Yo, you lying ya ass off. I ain't never cried for no bitch while I was snoozing. Say word if I did?"

Booker started to piss. "Word, nigga. The bitch name is Olivia. Now how would I know that shit right there?"

Scorpion cursed out loud. "Yeah, well that's my cousin's name. Me and her was real tight."

Booker laughed. "Oh yeah, I had a few cousins out in the Bronx that were tight with me like that. Some of the best pussies I ever had, so there definitely ain't no judgment coming from this direction. That family sex be hitting, word up." Booker shook off his dick and put it away. He flushed the toilet and was about to hop in the bed.

"Yo, nigga, wash ya hands, wit'cho nasty ass. Yo, I swear you Bronx niggas is grimy," Scorpion snapped, looking at Booker with disgust.

Booker turned around and ran water over his fingers with no soap. He wiped them on a white face towel that hung by the foot of their bunks. "Nigga, my dick is cleaner than my hands 'cause it don't touch nothing, yet my hands touch everything. So in essence, I should be trying to wash my joint off 'cause my hands touched it. Besides all that, you already know I go to court tomorrow for my last day of trial, right?"

"Yeah, but fuck that got to do with me?" Scorpion lay on his back, staring up at the bottom of Booker's prison bed.

"Nigga, if I lose, I'ma help you get up out of here like right away, that's my word to the Heavens."

Scorpion sat up. "Shut the fuck up, nigga. How you gon' do that? Keep in mind all that smoke blowing will get yo' ass smoked."

Booker laughed. "Yeah, yeah, nigga, all of that." He wiped his mouth. "You do know what they trying to book me on, right?"

Scorpion shook his head. "They don't let you choose yo' cellies here, my nigga, so I never wanna know what a nigga did to get put in this bitch, 'cause it'll make me look at you different."

"So then you don't?"

Scorpion shook his head. 'Somethin' federal, that's all I know."

"Then you don't know much." Booker grabbed a piece of paper that had traces of heroin on it. He hurried and took his work after the guard walked past and shot up the remaining amount that Scorpion had sold him only hours prior. He sat on the toilet and nodded in and out for ten minutes before he became lucid enough to talk. "Yo, I like those li'l white girls, Scorpion. I can't help it, B. Just something about they li'l ass drive me nuts, word up."

Scorpion raised his left eyebrow. "Okay, nigga. Why you telling me this?"

Booker nodded for a moment, snorting loudly, rocking back and forth. He closed his eyes. "They got me on trial saying that I kidnapped over eight girls, killed them, and buried their bodies from New York all the way up to Maine. They are trying to kill me, Scorpion. They said if I'm found guilty, the only way I can avoid the needle is if I give them the locations of three of the girls. They were socialites, real spoiled, pussies real tight." He groaned.

Scorpion hopped up and pointed at him, disgusted. "Bitch nigga, you better have a damn good reason for capping off right now. Talkin' like that about babies. Fuck is you on?"

Booker ran his hand over his face again. "Long story short, I ain't giving them shit. If I lose tomorrow and you can come up with twenty gees, I'ma give you the locations and the full rundown on what took place with four of the girls. All white, all rich, you should be able to work with that."

Scorpion felt his heart beating faster and faster. "Yo, why don't I just give you that cash anyway and we make this happen?"

Booker leaned forward in a daze until his face was inside of his lap. He snoozed for a moment, and then jerked awake. "Nah, nigga, let me see what's happening with me first, then you. Yo, but hit me with another round, Blood, word up, now you got me stressing." He smacked his lips together and smiled up at Scorpion.

Scorpion dipped into his stash and supplied him with a full gram that would have usually cost him every bit of four hundred dollars. "Yo, this is you, my dude, but you better be a man of yo' word, 'cause if you ain't, we're about to have some major problems."

Booker snatched the dope and mugged him for a moment. "Blood, you don't get it do you?" He stood up and looked directly into Scorpion's eyes. "I'm facing the death penalty in three states. I'm guaranteed to get at least three life sentences with no possibly of parole. There ain't shit that you can do to me that I ain't already did to myself. This next move on my behalf is a blessing 'cause you seem like a good nigga, and you been one hunnit ever since we been cellies, but please don't get shit twisted, I get down DOWN for this Blood shit.

Nah mean?" He stared into his eyes for a while before sitting down and getting his works together. "Yeah, B, this shit saucing. Court ain't gon' fuck with me long as I got this shit in my system. Good shit, Dunn, word the fuck up on that."

Scorpion sat on the edge of his bed and ran his hands over his face. "Yeah, a'ight, Booker, good luck tomorrow, god. I mean that with absolutely sincerity." Even though he really didn't. Although it was foul as fuck, he prayed that Booker lost his trial. He knew for certain that the knowledge that he was about to receive from him would be more than enough to get his sentence reduced or even thrown out. He closed his eyes and tried his best to get to sleep with Olivia captivating his mind constantly.

No matter how many times Scorpion tried to deny it, the fact was his brother and his fiancée were fucking around. Using his contraband cell phone, he hit up Othman, who texted him pictures of Paperchase and Olivia entering different hotels together and even footage of them having sex. Scorpion CashApp'ed him three gees by way of an apology for jumping on him that day he'd visited.

Chapter 9

Now that Scorpion had proof of Olivia's infidelity, he was determined to have her and his brother crushed. He'd placed a call to a reputable assassin that hailed from the notorious Parkway Garden Homes, locally known as O-Block on the South Side of Chicago. The steppa was a local legend that went by Justice, which was short for Street Justice. Scorpion had flown the young nigga out first class, got him a rental, put him up in a Four Seasons hotel and arranged to have the guns delivered to him he'd need for the assignment.

The job would be rather easy for Justice since he had a list of addresses where he could find Paperchase and Olivia. One night he followed them in Downtown New York where they'd paid for valet parking and entered through the doors of a five star Italian restaurant he couldn't pronounce. They carried on through dinner like a lovely young couple. From the outside looking in no one would have ever known that the two trifling motherfuckas were creeping behind Scorpions back.

When Justice saw the waiter bring them the bill, he put up the binoculars he'd been using to spy on them. He whistled as he pulled a pair of black latex gloves over his hands and made sure they were snug. He picked up the rubber clown mask lying on the passenger seat beside his burnout cell phone. He was about to slip the mask over his face when his cell suddenly rang. He was about to let that bitch keep ringing until he saw it was the man that had commissioned him for the hit calling him. Justice attached the voice distortion device onto the end of his cellular to disguise his voice before taking the call.

"Hello?" Justice asked, holding the cell to his ear and watching Paperchase cough up the bread for the meal.

"Say, bruh, you made that move yet?" Scorpion asked.

"Nah. I'm in the middle of that right now. Why? What's up?"

"Fall back."

"Fall back?"

"Yeah, B, fall back. I'm calling the whole thing off."

Justice was silent for a moment, watching Paperchase and Olivia leaving the restaurant holding hands, kissing. He shook his head like *these mothafuckas ain't shit.* He despised disloyalty, so much so he started to hop out and do them regardless of what Scorpion said. If it wasn't for the fact that he believed in never doing anything for free that you were good at, he definitely would have hopped out and did his shit.

"You do know there aren't any refunds, right?"

"I know. I forfeit the deposit, and I've gotta fork over your other half."

"These are facts."

"A'ight. I'ma have my people shoot chu that now."

Justice hung up, removed the device from his burnout cellular, and concealed his .45 automatic with the silencer inside of the stash spot. He watched Paperchase and Olivia make out as they waited for the valet to return with their car. He took the liberty to light up the half of a Dutch Master he'd been smoking earlier, cranked up the rental, and then drove off.

Paperchase had gotten a text from Scorpion telling him to wire a certain amount of money to an account as soon as possible. Paperchase would do as he was told before reserving a hotel for him and Olivia. Unbeknownst to him, he'd just dropped a bag on the man who was to be his executioner.

Scorpion powered off his cell phone and stashed it where he'd hidden it. He was thankful that he was able to call off the hit on his fiancée and his brother. He realized at the last minute he'd let his emotions get the best of him and he was going to make a decision that would cost him. He came to the conclusion that having his brother's head knocked off would ruin his chances of getting a sit-down with the plug. That new shit, the Rebirth, which Paperchase had hit him with had the niggas behind the walls going crazy. They couldn't get enough of it and they were sweating him for more.

To have his brother taken off his feet would be a decision he made out of his feelings. He reasoned that bitches dealt with situations in that manner and he wasn't a bitch. He made up his mind that he was going to act like shit was all good with baby bro when he touched the turf, get a meeting with whomever homeboy was hitting him with the Rebirth, negotiate a profitable deal, and then he was stinking his punk-ass brother and his smut-ass fiancée.

***

"Open cell thirty-seven, please!" The heavy set Mexican guard waited ten seconds before Scorpion and Booker's cell popped. As soon as it did, he ushered Booker inside of it and slammed the gate so hard that Scorpion's coffee mug fell off of the edge of the sink and crashed into the floor. He looked down at it and then trailed his eyes up to meet those of Booker's. He smiled.

"What the fuck you got that stupid-ass look on yo' face for?" Booker asked as Scorpion began to clean up the mess.

"Why are you mad at me? I don't know what you thought you were going to get. All of those little girls, the displaced families because of you... Did you think you were going to get found anything other than guilty?" the guard asked with a sneer on his face.

"Bitch, don't worry about it, just walk off before you get yourself in trouble," Booker warned.

The guard stepped closer to the gate. "Hey! I ain't no little white girl, Booker. You can't take advantage of me like you did them. I'll murder you first, you predator."

"Aw yeah? Well, you see, I know all about you. I know about yo' place in Staten Island. Your timeshare in Fort Lauderdale. I know what school your two daughters go to, and what they look like when they go swimming, all young and fresh and shit. Bitch, I'm not the one to play with. If I want those li'l bitches bad enough I'll get to 'em - if not me, somebody very close. You digging that, Jack?"

The guard backed away from the gate. "Yeah, Booker, well it ain't all about nothing, so let's just let bygones be bygones." He slowly backed away until he was off of their gallery.

As soon as he left, Booker slid down the bars and lowered his head into his lap. "Damn, I didn't think it would hurt this much to lose."

Scorpion handed him a tiny bag of Rebirth. "Huh, man, take the edge off. I take it we got a lot to talk about?"

Booker nodded. "Not much. I need forty gees and I'll give you three burial sites of politicians' daughters. They'll commute your sentence for these, I'm sure. Make it happen. I need a few days to just get high, and to figure out how I'm going to avoid the needle." He climbed from the floor and put up the sheet.

For the rest of the night, he shot up the dope while Scorpion lay back with his arms behind his head and a big smile on his face. Come hell or high water, he was going to find a way to use Booker's misfortune to get home. He was so close to getting his freedom he could reach out and touch it!

Chapter 10

Olivia sat and waited nervously for Scorpion to walk through the door of the visiting room. It was more than a hundred and ten degrees inside of it, and for some reason the guards had refused to turn the air conditioning system on to grant either the inmates or the visitors any sense of relief from the dreadful humidity that covered the atmosphere. While Olivia had been accustomed to wearing clothing that would keep Scorpion reminded of what he had out there on the streets waiting for him, this day she was dressed more modestly with a Yves St. Laurent skirt dress that hugged her frame just right. There was a slight, barely noticeable pudge in her midsection but to an untrained eye, or to a person that didn't know, it simply looked as if she was full from eating. She rubbed her hands together and kept her eyes trained on the door that Scorpion was sure to come through.

Paperchase came from the back of the visiting room and covered the entire table with food, and soft drinks. There was a variety of items that ranged from big-ass cheeseburgers to chicken sandwiches, down to a Snickers candy bar. There was a plethora of consumables with the exception of any swine products.

"Damn, babe, you for sure went all out. You sho' you spent enough cake on his food?" Olivia asked, rubbing her sweaty palms on the lap of her dress.

"Yo, cut that babe shit out, Liv. You gon' fuck around and slip up and say that shit in front of my brother and me and him gon' wind up tearing this visiting room up. I ain't trying to be bearing arms like that against my blood, nah mean?"

She sucked her teeth, "Yeah. I guess I do. But I really wanna know what you're going to do when he finally finds out that you and I are having a baby?"

Paperchase glanced toward the door and sat down. "I don't know, but now is neither the time nor the place. We came to give him some support and to find out if he has anything else lined up for us to assist him in getting up out of there anytime sooner. That's it; that's all."

Olivia rubbed her stomach. She felt it growl. The food on the table was starting to look good. She thought about mixing the Snicker with a bite of the chicken sandwich, but then the reality of her having to pee screamed at her. "Yeah, I got you, but right now I gotta pee. I'll be right back." She hopped up and scurried off toward the guard station for the restroom key, and then straight to the bathroom.

Paperchase exhaled loudly as he watched her ass jiggle as she made her journey toward the land of relief. He gazed around the visiting room and noted that it looked like baby mama central. There were women everywhere either with the men they came to see or waiting for them along with children all over the place. No matter where he looked, he saw that everybody was wiping sweat from their brow or popping their shirt to get some sort of relief from the hot conditions. He fanned his face with his hand and closed his eyes for a brief second. When he opened them, Scorpion was standing over him with a solemn look plastered across his handsome face. Paperchase jumped a bit and then gained his composure. "Fuck you sneaking up on the god like that for Dunn? Damn." He stood up to embrace his brother.

Scorpion laughed, "Yo you lacking, Pa. The streets out there must be getting nice. Word up, I stayed on edge from the opps. A nigga could have never slid on me like I just did you." He hugged his little brother and patted his back. Over his shoulder, his facial expression was that of an angry murderer. When he stepped back to look into Paperchase's face again, he was back smiling. "Where my bitch at?"

Paperchase grimaced for a second upon hearing his brother calling Olivia out of her name. It angered him, and then he remembered that Olivia technically belonged to Scorpion as far as his brother knew. "She had to piss. You already know how this atmosphere gets her li'l ass and all that shit."

"Yo, she better hurry up before they start talking like I won't be able to get my initial embrace from her and shit. They just lifted our mask mandate, so for the god, it's long overdue." He rubbernecked and looked to the back by the bathrooms, then decided she'd be a minute, so he took a seat.

"Yo, so what's the good news? Why you wanted us to come out here all abrupt and shit?" Paperchase asked, grabbing an orange juice. The Percocet had him feeling dehydrated like never before.

"It's a surprise, nigga, but I wanna wait until Olivia get here so I can tell both of y'all at the same time." He pointed at the apple juice and Paperchase nodded his head to indicate that it was for him and so was everything else on the table.

"Yo, so the news is that good, huh killa?" Paperchase drank half of the juice and burped.

"I thank so. Man, this bitch taking forever, I'm 'bout to have you go and get her ass if she stays in that muthafucka one more minute. Fuck taking her so long?"

Paperchase shrugged his shoulders. "Chill, B, we got three and a half hours. It's all good."

Scorpion scoffed. "Aw, so now you telling me what to do?"

Paperchase looked off and then pointed. "There she goes right there. You can cool ya jets now, boss."

Olivia strutted over, looking ten times as fine to Scorpion as she ever had, and it was crazy because she was without makeup or a bunch of long pointless fingernails. She was fresh faced with her hair pulled back into a ponytail. "What did I miss?"

Scorpion stood up and stepped in front of her. "Hey baby, long time no see. How is my ride or die bitch?" He slipped his fingers behind her neck, ready to tongue her down.

Olivia knew what was coming already. She sort of recoiled, and side stepped him. "Scorpion, I ain't feeling that bitch word no more. I'm more than that now."

"What? Since when?" He mugged Paperchase.

Paperchase looked off. "Yo, now I gotta hit the head. I'ma let y'all get acquainted and I'll be back in a minute." He walked away from the pair.

Olivia waited until Paperchase was out of sight before she allowed herself to be kissed by Scorpion. He took full advantage too. He slipped his tongue into her mouth and grabbed ahold of her ass while giving her sexual audio. She tried to step back and he pulled her even closer. After two full minutes, he released her and they sat.

Olivia crossed her thighs and wiped his kisses from her lips. She took a carton of orange juice and drank from it to get the taste of him off of her tongue. "So how have you been?"

"Yo, did you just wipe my kiss away?" Scorpion scooted to the edge of his seat, feeling his stomach turning over and over from her actions.

"What? Nah, I wasn't even thinking about that. I just wiped my mouth. It had nothing to do with your kisses."

"Yeah. Whatever, bitch. I saw that shit as clear as day. But fuck you though." He wiped sweat from his face. "You fuckin' off, ain't you?"

"What? I know damn well you ain't call me all the way up here for this shit?" She crossed her arms. *Where the hell is Paperchase?* she thought.

Scorpion popped her on the side of the knee, too hard to be joking, and not hard enough to be an assault. "Keep that shit a buck with me. You fuckin' off with another nigga, ain't you?"

Olivia stood up. "Scorpion, we grown as hell. I ain't come down here to discuss my personal business. I came to make sure that you were good. Why can't we chill for the little time we have together without arguing? It seem like that's all we've been doing lately."

Scorpion nodded. "I get it. Nigga been gone for almost two years now. They gave me damn near life, and there really ain't no ending to this time in sight, so why wouldn't you fuck off? I mean, that's common sense. It's good though." He rubbed her knee for a moment, and then stopped. "Never count me out though, bitch. That's the worst thang you could ever do. When you do that shit, it turns you into the opp. Just know that."

"Yo, you tripping. I still love yo' ass, but you just been tripping for the past few weeks. Hopefully, you ain't got that Corona shit, but somethin' ain't right." She sat back down and started to look for Paperchase.

He laughed. "Yeah, shorty, maybe it's just that. Or maybe I know more than what the fuck you thank I know. You ever think about that!" He raised his voice.

Olivia stood up. "That's it; I'm up outta here. I ain't got time to be arguing with you. Call me later."

Scorpion stood up and grabbed her arm, "Bitch, if you walk away from me, I can't be held responsible for what I do to yo' ass. You already know how I get down."

Olivia snatched her arm away from him and thought about all the times that Scorpion had beat her into submission. Suddenly, she was filled with anger. "You know what, Scorpion? Do what you gotta do. I ain't scared of you no more. I'm out of here. Bye!" As she was walking away, Paperchase was coming toward them. She walked right into his face. "I can't do this with him anymore, baby. I love you too much. I'll be down in the Bentley. Hurry up before they ask me to leave the parking lot." She walked away from him.

Paperchase and Scorpion locked eyes.

Chapter 11

"You wanna tell me why she acting all funny toward me and shit, or should I get to just assuming some other fuck shit?" Scorpion asked as he took his seat and started to work on his juice again.

Paperchase sat and sighed. "I don't know, bruh. She probably PMS'ing or somethin'." He avoided eye contact with Scorpion and tried to think of another subject that would help them to cruise the last two hours of his visit. "But don't let what she's got going on ruin yo' good news. Tell me what it do?"

Scorpion stood up, "Nah, it's good. I don't wanna talk about that shit no more. Honestly, I need to get my mind right. That bitch got me emotionally lacking and I ain't feeling that. I gotta get a hold of myself. All I need for you to do is to keep handling bidness as usual. I'll figure everything else out. It's all good with the clan, right?"

Paperchase nodded, "Yeah, I'm fuckin' with the plug the long way. He has a list of demands before he makes that Rebirth shit happen, but I'm on top of it. I'll be back to holler at you once everything is finalized, until then I'ma keep hitting yo' books and holding you down. That's my word."

Scorpion laughed. "Li'l bruh, in most cases it's never a man's word that gets him into trouble, but his loyalty. Keep me in tune. Woo out, my nigga. Gang Gang." He waved to the guards and stormed out of the door with anger coursing through him worse than ever before. Within his heart and within his mind Olivia had broken bad and the reality was almost enough to shatter him.

Just wait 'til a nigga come home. I'ma regulate shit and the whole nine, son.

***

Toya held Ramone's hand as they stood over Jayshawn's casket. Tears rolled down his face and dripped onto Jayshawn's silk shirt, staining it. There were only three other people inside of the funeral home. Two of them Ramone didn't know, and the other person was the mortician. Toya had chosen to wear a stunning red dress and black Christian Louboutin red bottoms. Ramone, on the other hand, adopted an all-black Chanel fit with black and gray Retro Jordans number eights. The Cartiers on his face hid his eyes from the indescribable pain that resonated deep within his soul. The mortician played the organ and with each chord that he struck Ramone found himself feeling sicker and sicker.

The door to the funeral home opened and Martha staggered inside with a bottle of Wild Irish Rose. She took a sip from the bottle and slipped into the back pew. She wore a gray jogging fit and sandals. Her eyes were red-webbed and glassy. She rubbed them with her fists and kept right on drinking.

Ramone glanced back at her and slumped his shoulders. His tears began to flow again as he looked down at his older brother lying inside of the coffin. "Damn, big bruh, why you? You were never on that type of time. Why did they have to take you?"

"Everything is gonna be okay, baby. I got you. We're in this together – forever," Toya told him, affectionately squeezing his hand.

Jabari came into the funeral home with two notorious shooters behind him. He slipped beside Martha and placed his arm around her shoulder. "Damn, ma, you smell real foul right now, but I get it. I'm sorry for your loss. Me and your oldest were jammed tight. That was my dawg. You ain't gotta worry about his murder going without revenge. I'ma take care of that shit, you betta believe it."

Martha was drunk out of her mind. She could only comprehend about fifty percent of what Jabari was saying. "Thank you, baby, but I got a good feeling that it's all in God's hands. We just have to let it work itself out." She hiccupped and belched right behind it.

Jabari slipped her an ounce of Afghan heroin. "Yo, this that fire right here and it's on the house. "Don't let Ramone know, okay?" He smirked and winked at her.

Martha tucked it into her jogging pants and then directly inside of her big panties that were so stained, even she was embarrassed at the sight of them. "Thank you, child. Lord knows this is just what I needed." She tried to hug him.

Jabari slid away and stood up. "Enough with all that. You still smell a way, shorty." He stepped into the aisle and walked towards Ramone.

Toya looked over her shoulder and saw Jabari approaching. She figured he'd want to have a moment with Ramone alone, so she decided to excuse herself. "Baby, I gotta use the restroom. I'll be right back, okay?" she said, running her fingers through his dreadlocks. Ramone nodded.

Toya kissed him on the side of his face and headed to the restroom. She waved "Hi" at Jabari and he smiled and waved back at her.

Jabari placed his hand on Ramone's right shoulder and shook his head. "We gotta get these niggas, B. Even though me and blood had our issues, I would have never let a nigga touch a hair on his head." He took his two fingers that he'd previously dipped in liquid soap and allowed to dry and then touched the inner corners of his eyes with them, causing tears to run out of them from the burning sensation. "Jayshawn was my nigga. Damn, I miss my dawg." He pulled Ramone to him and hugged the young gunner.

Ramone broke down all the way, crying into Jabari's embrace. "They took my brother, dawg. Them niggas had the nerve to murder Jayshawn because of some shit my mother owed them and she won't even tell me who they are. Ain't that some shit?" Ramone looked over his shoulder to see that Martha had already left out of the door again after not having paid her last respects to her son. He felt a little bit of love leave his system toward her.

"Yo, that shit doesn't even matter because I already know who dropped Jayshawn - or at least I know who gave the order," Jabari said, wiping his cheeks. He leaned over and touched Jayshawn's chest. "Rest in heaven, my nigga. God's speed."

Ramone looked up at him, "Are you serious? You really know who gave the order for his hit?"

"Nigga, you already know that I am the streets. Ain't shit taking place in New York without me knowing about it."

"Awright, then spit it out. Who gave the order?" Ramone was exceedingly angry. He needed to know. The suspense was literally eating away at him.

Jabari placed his arm around his neck again. "I'ma break down everything for you, kid, right after we put yo' brother in the dirt. I got a few pallbearers back there and we gon' send the kid off right, and then you and I are going to talk bidness. But first things is first." He tapped Jayshawn's casket at the closed foot portion of it. "Let's get the homie squared away."

***

Paperchase waited until Olivia stepped inside of the hotel room before he slammed the door behind her. The sudden noise caused her to jump. Paperchase stepped into her face. "What the fuck was all that about, Liv?"

Olivia ran her fingers through her curly hair after removing her ponytail and walking away from him. "Excuse me for loving yo' ass so much that I can no longer fake the funk with yo' brother. The fact that I even had to kiss him was enough to almost make me throw up. I ain't feeling that no more, and I ain't feeling you always jumping on me for living my truths neither." She walked into the bathroom.

Paperchase was right behind her on her heels. "I thought we decided that when we told him what it was that we were going to tell him together?"

"We did, and I didn't say nothing. So what's the problem?" She turned around and bumped him out of the way.

Paperchase held his composure. "The problem is that it doesn't take much for Scorpion to get wind of us. That nigga ain't stupid. This is the first time that you've been in his presence acting all stuck up and shit and it doesn't help that I was right there with you looking like a damn fool." He followed her into the room.

She walked back past him and went into the bathroom. She pulled up her skirt and sat on the toilet, peeing away. "Yo I can't fake the funk no more. You can take it how you want to. I got yo' seed inside of me and that's just what it is. That nigga finna have to find out what it is sooner or later anyway. I'm not understanding the problem." She finished her due, flushed, got up, and washed her hands. She nudged past him once again. This time she sat on the bed and took her heels off. "Uhh, damn that feels good. Yo, I don't know how much longer I'ma be rocking heels and all of that shit neither. My puppies are barking. You gon' rub my feet for me? After all, I'm your baby mother." She smiled at that and held her slender feet in the air.

Paperchase stood on the side of the bed, shaking his head. "You thank this shit is a game, don't you?"

She smacked her lips. "Aww, why would you say that?" She rolled her eyes. "Nigga, this is us. Sooner or later he gon' know what it is anyway. Scorpion got life to do. You would thank he would want me to carry on with his brother instead of some other nigga. That only seems quite natural." She wiggled her toes. "You got me or what?"

Paperchase dropped his head and sat on the bed. He took her left foot and started to rub it. Olivia lay back with her eyes closed, in heaven. Paperchase sighed, imagining him and Scorpion one day exchanging gunfire over Olivia. He shook his head in sickness. "Yo, I love my brother. I don't know what it is about yo' ass, but you got me twisted, Olivia. You are too deep inside of my soul already and I ain't feeling this shit. I gotta shake you, goddess, word up."

Chapter 12

Olivia took her foot out of his hand and crawled across the bed. She pushed him back and straddled his lap. She kissed his lips, noting how much bigger and softer they were in comparison to Scorpion's. "Listen here, baby daddy, it ain't meant for you to shake me. Everything happens for a reason. I'm yours now and you are mine. That's just what it is, and the world has to accept that. The world includes Scorpion. Man up; that's all I can tell you." She kissed his lips again and climbed off of him, sitting on the edge of the bed with her head down.

Paperchase sat on the bed for a moment and then he slid off of it and knelt before her. He looked up at her and noticed that she avoided staring down at him and this made him exhale slowly. "Baby, look at me."

Olivia refused for a moment, then slowly she looked down at him almost irritably. "What's up, Paperchase?"

Paperchase was serious. "Baby, I love you. I don't know how or when it happened, and I swear I feel bogus as hell for stabbing my brother in the back on this level, but I can't deny how much I really love you. I think I always felt this way about you even before you decided to cross over to me, as much as I hate to admit that shit right there, but it's the truth." He lowered his head and got lost in thought for a moment. "I need to face Scorpion and let him know what it is, I know I do, but how the fuck do I do that, ma? My brother always been there for me." His eyes became misty before he frowned and forced the cold-hearted killer side of him to push its way to the forefront.

Olivia nodded in understanding. "It's not easy for me either, baby. Your brother was all I ever knew. It didn't matter how brazen or tough I've always acted because when it all boils down, I'm just a fragile female that ain't afraid to buss her gun for the man and for the crew that I love. To be honest, my eyes have always been on you. I've always thought you were the most handsome, the most laid back, the most intelligent, and the most caring and loving toward me. I have been feeling you, so I think this what we have has always been inevitable. I think we might have been kidding ourselves thinking that this would have never popped off. At least that's how I feel." She stroked the side of his face.

Tears dropped from his eye wells now. "Not if he was here. I would have never gone behind his back like this. Even though I have always found you hot as hell, I knew where my place was. I knew I shouldn't be peeping ya curves, ya walk, huffing ya scent, and all of that good shit that makes my joints twitch. Yo, I ignored that goddess, but now I can't. I ain't got the discipline to, and what does that say about my loyalty for my kinfolk?" He lowered his head again. "Damn, I ain't right."

She slipped off of the bed and wrapped her arms around his neck. "Baby, you can't be looking at it like that. You have to follow your own heart for once. As long as I have known you, you've always been about following Scorpion's every order, or doing things to strengthen your borough. It's never been about you. I am the first thing that you've made out for yourself and that's okay because I love you just as much as you love me. Probably more."

"But at what expense and at whose expense?" The tears dripped off of his chin just as his nose began to run.

Now Olivia was crying. "All I know is that we deserve this. It may have started as a pastime because the both of us were lost due to Scorpion's absence because he had been giving us orders for so long, but now I know that our love is real and we need to enjoy and be thankful for it. Now I'm down for you. All I need to know is if you're down for me just as hard."

Paperchase nodded. "Yeah, boo. I am."

Olivia smiled and started to shake. "A'ight den, it's time we embrace that Scorpion is gone and that it's me and you, and this baby. We need to get our ducks in a row and get our paper together so that we can go and do the family thing. What do you say?"

Paperchase made her stand up. He tilted her chin upward and kissed her lips. "A'ight, baby, I gotta get out here and check this bag for us. I'm thinking about ten mill and then we can leave New York and start our life together with our baby. I gotta get out here though. There ain't no other way."

She nodded in understanding. "I get it, and I know what has to be done. I wish we could just run off together and figure things out as we go along, but I think that our child will need more than a head start in life. I always know that whenever a couple gets close to being loved and in love the right way that it seems like all sorts of road blocks come out of nowhere. We can't allow for that to happen to us. We have to handle bidness and get out of New York. That's the only way that this will work. Do you get that?"

"Yeah, boo, I do." He exhaled slowly and loudly. He slipped his hand under her shirt and rubbed her belly. "I gotta make it happen, not only for us, but for this gift right here. So that's what I'ma do."

"I got you too. No matter what happens, or where we go, or what we go through, I got you. I mean that with all of my heart and soul." She hugged him tightly. "I love you, baby."

Paperchase took a short moment, and then squeezed her. "I love you too, yo. This is our new normal."

***

"One thing I need for you to know is that when it comes to the game, any snitching will get yo' ass dropped faster than a prom date that ain't trying to fuck after the last dance. But I got mad love for you, and I can't have you walking around New York in a daze like a chicken with yo' head cut off. I gotta let you know exactly what it is." Jabari said this before he leaned forward and tooted up two thin lines of heroin that was imported directly from Afghanistan.

The basement was just above ninety degrees. It was hot and sticky with bugs crawling all around it. Ramone wiped the sweat off of his brow and tried his best to sit upright. The heroin had him higher than he had ever been. He could barely open his eyes, and on top of that, there felt like there were bugs all over him, causing him to dig deep into his skin before he scratched blood out of himself. "Yo, I get all of that, but let me know what the bidness is and I'll handle this shit as I see fit."

Jabari was laid back against the cushions, snoring and scratching at the same time. Though it appeared that he was asleep, he'd heard every word that Ramone had uttered. "Yo, you my li'l nigga and I ain't about to let you do shit on yo' own without assisting you. But I'ma let you know what's to it." He ran his hand over his face. "It's Paperchase. That nigga done had it out for Jayshawn for years now. Before I took a liking to you, li'l homie, all that fool talked about was drilling yo' brother. I knew it was gon' happen sooner or later. I guess Jayshawn owed that nigga some cake and they'd gotten into a few disputes over the last few weeks. But that's that bidness right there."

Ramone hopped up. "So you mean to tell me that the same nigga that popped me kilt my brother too?" He staggered on his feet. His eyes looked as if they belonged to an Asian. He could just barely open them.

Jabari stood up and nodded. "We gon' get his ass though, me and you. Just keep ya tool kit and I'ma make sure we drill that nigga real nicely."

"I wanna know where his mother stay. Where is his baby mother, his kid? I wanna make that bitch feel just as bad as I do right now," Ramone said, cocking his gun. The sound of a live round entering the banger's chamber resonated inside of the basement.

Jabari smiled and licked his lips. "In due time, god. Trust me. What I got planned, you'll be feeling a whole lot better when it's all said and done. That's my word."

"A'ight, bruh, I'm finna raise up outta here." Ramone stood up, lifting his hand.

"Hold up, King. I'm not finished hollerin' at chu yet." Jabari motioned for him to sit down and he did. "Remember I told you about that product that was gon' change our lives, and have us white man rich?" Ramone nodded. "Well, this shit is called Rebirth. It's genetically engineered so a fiend can never get off it. Anyway, I've got footage of a fiend's reaction to it." He clapped his hands.

Instantly, two of his demons, Spank and Jibbs, emerged from somewhere deep inside of the basement, rolling out something covered in a sheet. Spank snatched off the sheet and revealed a 30-inch flat screen television set with remote control. Jibbs picked up the remote control and handed it to Jabari.

"Good lookin' out," Jabari told him. He sat on the table and turned on the television with the remote control. He then activated the play option on the DVD player.

The TV popped on, displaying a scrawny dopefiend with half his head braided in frizzy cornrows. He was on his knees inside of an undisclosed area with a belt wrapped around his arm. He clenched a syringe full of dope between his teeth and tapped his arm until a vein became pronounced. He pushed the drug into his system and smiled happily as it took effect. As the days went by, the dopefiend became sick as fuck, throwing up and shitting everywhere. He was told he'd get a gram of the Rebirth with every task he completed. He completed them all. He'd eaten a rodent, human feces, performed fellatio on a stray dog, gouged out his own eye, and finally chopped off his left arm. A masked man came inside the room he was being held in and stopped the bleeding. He put the junkie's severed arm inside of a cooler filled with ice and then gave him a shot of dope.

After the footage had ended, Jabari turned the television set off and motioned for his demons to store it away. He then turned around to Ramone, who looked shocked at what he had just seen.

"You see that shit, bruh? Muthafuckas are willing to do anything and everything for this Rebirth. We've gotta game changer on our hands."

"You ain't never lied." Ramone nodded. If he wasn't before, he was definitely sold on trafficking this new narcotic Jabari was talking about.

"All you gotta do is get bruh out the way. Then two more niggas, and we're set to take over all of Brooklyn." Jabari assured him. "Nah, fuck that. We'll be set to take over all five boroughs."

Chapter 13

Booker's people on the outside let him know that the 40 gees had been deposited into his account and he gave Scorpion the locations of the three dead white girls. Scorpion had a sit-down with the warden of the facility and he got in touch with the daughters of the politicians. They agreed to Scorpion's proposal and had their attorney draw up the paperwork. Scorpion had his attorney look over the documents to make sure he wouldn't get fucked in the deal. Once his attorney confirmed that everything was legit, he signed his John Hancock beside the X. The ink hadn't had time to dry before the authorities got to work digging up the burial sites of the corpses.

A half dozen of New York City's Finest wore Coronavirus masks as they stood around talking and watching two men shoveling up the ground. There were three halogen LED work lights with adjustable metal telescoping tripods focused on the five foot deep ditch that was being dug. The two men, who wore trucker caps, lower facial coverings, and navy blue jumpsuits, breathed heavily and grunted as they performed the task at hand. They'd been at it for hours, but they both had vowed to the little white girls' parents that they wouldn't stop that night until they uncovered their child's burial site - if she was truly where they were informed she'd be.

The mothers and fathers stood on the opposite side of the ditch from the police. They were hugged snuggly in the arms of their husbands while watching the ditchdigger's hard at work. Tears twinkled in the eyes of the wives and some of the husbands blinked back theirs. They were the pillars of strength in their families, so they had to remain strong. All of the couples' hearts raced, wondering which of their little girls would be found first. Having their kid's body uncovered would be bitter-sweet, but finally being able to lay them to rest properly would provide them with some kind of comfort.

"Jesus Christ, my fucking back is killing me," one of the ditch diggers said, taking a break from digging while his partner continued with the task they were given. He was a fiftyish white man with a graying mustache that curled over his top lip. He pulled the covering down from over the lower half of his face and wiped his sweaty, dirt smudged face with the back of his gloved hand. "Say, you boys got any more of those cold ones up there?" he called up from the ditch towards where the cops were standing.

"Yeah. There's plenty. We've got an entire chest full!" an older officer yelled down inside of the ditch while peering over into it. He had a meaty hand on his hip while the other one was holding a hot cup of coffee with steam billowing from it.

"Well, would'ja be a pal and toss me one down?" he asked, then looked to the other ditch digger and asked if he wanted one.

"No, thanks. I told myself I'll have my next brew once I give one of these families closure by delivering the remains of their little girl," the partner replied, huffing and puffing while shoveling up the earth. Sweat poured down his back and face, but he was determined to deliver what he'd promised.

"How noble of you. Say, pal, just one." The ditch digger held up a finger to the cop. He nodded understandingly, retrieved a beer from the cooler, and then tossed it down to the ditch digger.

The ditch digger caught it, thanked the cop, who gave him a thumbs up, and then he popped the cap off with an opener on his key ring. He took the bottle to the head, guzzling it thirstily, and throat rolling up and down his neck. He brought the bottle down, wiped his dripping lips, and belched.

"I think I've found something!" the other ditch digger announced, tossing his shovel aside.

The cops and the families surrounded the ditch looking down. The ditch digger who'd been drinking the beer set it aside and bent down beside the other. A black garbage bag with dirt residue on it was partially submerged in the ground. They cleared the rest of the dirt from around the garbage bag. Everyone looked on as the ditch digger who'd announced his findings began to tear open the head of the bag. It was cold and silent. The families were on edge, listening to their hearts pounding within their ears and holding each other tighter. One of the mothers closed her eyes, and tears slid down her cheeks. She clutched the crucifix hanging around her neck and said a silent prayer.

The ditch digger tore open the black garbage bag and revealed the greenish-blue, decomposing face of a seven-year-old white girl. Her eyes were a cloudy light-blue and sunken into her sockets. The skeletal bone structure of his temples and face were pronounced.

Frowning from the god awful smell coming from the dead body, the ditchdigger's held their gloved hands over their noses and mouths while taking a step backwards. It was the best they could do to keep from puking everywhere.

"Oh my God, no! That's her! That's our baby! That's our Caroline!" one of the mothers cried out with tears bursting from her eyes. She went to jump down inside of the ditch, but her husband snagged her arm. He pulled her into him, and she desperately tried to fight him off.

The surrounding officers shook their heads pityingly and some of them even crossed themselves with the holy crucifix. Their hearts went out to the mother and father of the little girl. They couldn't fathom the way they must have been feeling in that moment and they didn't want to either.

The grieving mother's fight against her husband grew slower and slower until she eventually stopped. She buried her tear streaked face into her daughter's father's chest, bawling long and loud. He hugged her tighter. His bottom lip trembled as tears threatened to spill down his cheeks. Finally, he couldn't fight his overwhelming sorrow, and his grief spilled out of his eyes.

"Nooooooo! God, why her? Why my darling Caro-liiiiine?" the mother bellowed with a voice riddled by pain from her devastating loss.

The other families held each other tighter. They felt the dead girl's parents' loss, and dreaded when the time came when it would be their child being dug up from an early grave.

***

A day later, in the wee hours of the morning, another pair of ditch diggers was shoveling up piles of dirt. In the beginning they'd use an excavator to dig up the ground, but once they'd concluded they'd gotten far enough below the surface, they switched to shoveling to complete the task. The men were wearing bandanas around the lower halves of their face to protect them from the deadly spread of the Coronavirus. Their faces were shiny from sweat while their jumpsuits were covered in smudges of dirt. Up on the surface, the police and the families of the girls that had been kidnapped, raped and murdered stood around, watching them. They were dressed warm to combat the weather, and wearing either a Coronavirus mask or some other facial covering.

"Alright. I think we've got something!" one of the ditch diggers called up to the surface. His announcement drew the police and the families closer to the ditch. They watched closely as the ditch diggers worked harder and faster to uncover their discovery.

Little by little, a greenish-blue hand, with yellowing grossly overgrown fingernails, emerged. When the ditch diggers finally got to the victim's face, which was fixed with the dead look, cloudy blue-eyes, and a mouth full of dirt, they heard a pained shriek cut through the air.

"It's-it's our granddaughter, Jo-Josephine!" a burly white man with graying hair croaked. Wincing, he staggered backwards, clutching the left side of his chest. He blinked his eyes ·rapidly and looked around like he didn't know where he was. He took a step back awkwardly and fell on his back, drawing the attention of everyone around him.

His wife, an elderly, portly woman with graying cherry-blonde hair, pulled her Coronavirus mask down from her nose and mouth, rushing toward him. A panicked look was on her face and there was worry in her eyes.

"Oh, my God, Thurston! What's the matter?" she asked, helping him to the ground. The other parents came to bend beside the older couple, wondering what was happening to the old man. The police started over toward them. One of them called in for an ambulance.

"I think-I think I'm-I'm having a-a heart attack!" Thurston gritted as he continued to clutch his chest.

"Dear, Lord, someone call an ambulance!" the old man's wife said out loud, looking around frantically while holding her husband's hand. One of the officers kneeled down beside him to check his well-being while another one hit up dispatch for an ambulance.

***

Mists of rain fell in blankets softening the mud, making the ground mushy. The red and blue lights perched on top of parked police cars spun around like disco balls, illuminating everyone in the vicinity. Police officers, a couple of detectives and ditch diggers stood around chopping it up while the coroners loaded a dead girl's body into the back of their van. The father of the little girl, Garette, focused his attention on the van until it disappeared into the crisp, cold night. He blinked back tears while holding an umbrella over his and his wife's head. Seeing their daughter's corpse made his wife's legs feel like cooked spaghetti noodles. She found it difficult to sustain her equilibrium, but thankfully, her husband was strong enough to keep her up.

"My baby, my baby, my Joann! Why'd it have to be her, Garette? Why'd it have to be our innocent little girl?" she cried out with a drenched cheeks and buried her face into his chest. The police tried to tend to her, but Garette shook his head at them. They knew then that he had everything under control so they backed off.

Garette was about to say something, but he could hear his voice crackling with emotions the moment he opened his mouth. He blinked back tears, took a deep breath and tried again. "Don't you worry, sweetheart. I'm gonna see to it that bastard gets the needle. I swear on our little girl's soul, that son of a bitch is gonna get his," Garette angrily promised his sobbing wife.

They'd just identified their seven-year-old daughter Joann. She'd been kidnapped, sexually assaulted, and murdered. Her body had decomposed so much that they couldn't tell that it was her until they saw the growth on the side of her hand. She'd had it since she was a baby, and they'd never gotten it surgically removed because the mother believed it was good

luck for some odd reason. But on this night, there wasn't anyone that could convince her that "good luck" wasn't a contra-
diction.

Ghost & Tranay Adams

Chapter 14

A glossy black 1969 Chevrolet Camaro hardtop ripped up the street, disturbing the debris. Money Moe, a brolic nigga who was as black as the Ace of Spades and had a head as wide as a Rottweiler, was behind the wheel. James Brown was blasting so loudly his sideview mirrors were trembling.

Moe bent a few more corners and made a right down a residential street. He made a left into the driveway of his red bricked house, parked in the backyard, and then locked the gate behind him. He popped the trunk of his classic vehicle and grabbed two duffle bags out of it. He used his elbow to slam the trunk closed and hustled over to the back door. As soon as he got inside of the crib, he kicked the door closed and locked it behind him. He could hear music playing from somewhere inside of the house.

Moe dumped the two duffle bags onto the dining room table, hung up his leather jacket, and removed the shoulder holsters that held his Desert Eagles. He hung his holsters on the back of one of the dining room table chairs and grabbed a beer from out of the refrigerator. He popped the cap on it and took a swig.

"Baby girl, what chu doing back there? It's time you get on the road before it gets too late," Moe called out to his daughter. She was usually the one to drop off the product to the cooks. He used her to move the shit since the police were less prone to pulling over female drivers.

When Moe didn't get a response, he listened closer to the music. He could hear Jodeci's "Come & Talk to Me". He set his beer down on the dining room table and made his way down the hallway. The closer he came to the music, the louder it became to him until he was at the bathroom door. He cracked open the door and peered inside. He licked his lips hungrily, seeing his daughter behind the shower curtain. It had been quite some time since he'd sampled her goodies. He'd smashed mad bitches during his stint as a crack king, but none of those broads had shit on his baby girl.

Moe knew fucking on your own flesh and blood was frowned upon, but it was something about that forbidden pussy that did something to him. Fucking someone you didn't have any business fucking really got his dopamine going. The taboo sex provided a high no drug on earth could compare to and he couldn't get enough of it.

Moe slipped his hand inside of his jeans and stroked his dick. He stroked his piece faster and faster, seeing a now naked Toya stepping out of the tub and drying herself off. She'd wrapped the towel around her bosom when he could no longer contain himself any longer and just had to have her.

"Fuck this," Moe said, kicking the door open. It banged off the bathroom wall and scared the hell out of Toya. Her eyes bucked and she placed her hand over her chest.

"Daddy, you scared the crap outta me."

"My bad, baby girl."

"It's okay. I was just finna head on out anyway."

Toya took a step towards the door and he stepped into her path.

"It's all good, baby girl. It's been a loooooong time since you and I spent a li'l father and daughter time together." Moe unbuckled his belt and unzipped his jeans. He pulled his meat out and started pumping it to its full potential.

Toya stepped back until she bumped up against the bathtub. She looked around and realized she was cornered as her father stalked toward her.

"Daddy, please no! I don't wanna do this. This ain't right!" Toya pleaded with tears sliding down her cheeks. Her heart was racing and she felt like she was going to throw up or faint maybe even both.

"I know, I know, but it feels so good, baby girl." His dick was as hard as a diving board and pre-cum was seeping out of its head. "I'll tell you what though. Just for the night, I won't fuck you if you promise to suck my big, black dick like you used to when you were little. How about that?"

By this time, Toya's face was drenched and her heart was beating so fast it felt like it would burst. Shorty was terrified, but her father didn't give a damn. The sick son of a bitch wanted what he wanted.

"Can you do that for daddy? Huh?" Moe asked in a low sensual voice caressing her cheek.

Toya shut her eyes and tears jetted down her cheeks. She fidgeted with her fingers, bowed her head, and conceded to what he wanted.

"That's my girl." He forced his tongue inside of her mouth and kissed her like he used to kiss her mother.

She tried to hide the look of disgust that came across her face, but she couldn't help it. She desperately wanted to vomit, but feared what he'd do if she actually did.

Moe removed her towel, took her by her hand, and slowly twirled her around like a ballerina. "My, my, my, my baby has grown. You're officially a grown-ass woman."

Toya whimpered as he lowered her to her knees. She snuck a glance up at the pole that held up the shower curtain. She knew it wasn't properly wedged between the walls so she had enough strength to pull it down. She was confident she could use it as a weapon.

"You know how daddy likes it," he told her as he ran his fingers through her hair. She nodded. "Well, tell me, baby. Tell me how daddy likes it."

"You-you like it slow with a lot of sp-spit," Toya stammered.

"That's right. Now go on and make daddy feel good." Moe smiled, closed his eyes, and tilted his head back. He couldn't wait to feel his daughter's mouth on the end of his piece. In his book, her dick sucking skills were phenomenal and second to none.

Toya spat on his piece a few times before she started pumping it with one hand. She kept an eye on him as she reached for the pole holding up the shower curtain.

"Damn, baby girl, what's taking you so——"

Moe was cut short when Toya punched him in his balls. He howled in pain and grabbed his precious jewels. She shoved him to the floor and dashed for the bathroom door. He grabbed her ankle and before she knew it, the floor was flying up at her face. Moe pulled up his jeans and made his way over to her on his knees. She turned over on her back and kicked him in the face three times, each kick harder than the last. Moe dropped to the floor with a bleeding nose and a busted mouth. Toya scrambled to her feet and took off running. Her tits bounced up and down and her ass cheeks jiggled.

"I'ma fucking-I'ma fucking kill you, bitch!" Moe swore between winces, touching his face and coming away with blood. "You don't ever raise yo' hand to me! I'm yo' fucking father!"

Moe got up from the floor and limped after Toya as fast as he could. He'd seen her running towards her bedroom and feared she may be going for a gun.

Toya fled to her bedroom, where she took a sheathed machete from the top shelf of her closet. She pulled the huge blade from its enclosure as Moe grabbed her from behind. At that moment, something within Toya's mind snapped. She swung the machete around and sliced her father's jugular. His

94

eyes bucked and blood spilled down his neck profusely. He grabbed his throat and plasma seeped between his fingers. He tried to say something, but the words wouldn't form. He reached out to Toya and she took another swipe at him, sending his severed hand flying across the bedroom. Blood gushed out of his stump and he looked at it disbelievingly. He looked back at Toya.

"You fucking bastard! I fucking hate chu, yo!" Toya shouted maniacally, tears pouring down her cheeks in buckets, snot peeking out of her nose. She threw the machete over her head and swung it down with all her might. As soon as the big blade collided with Moe's forehead, blood splattered against her face and made her look like a psychopath.

Moe collapsed to the floor. Toya placed her foot on his chest and yanked the machete out of his skull with two quick tugs. She nearly fell when she pulled the machete loose. Straddling his waist, she brought the machete above her head again. Her mind was assault with visual after visual of her father violently raping her over and over again. Her head trembled, her body shook, her eyes bulged and the veins covering her forehead threatened to explode.

"How could you do what you did to me, Daddy? How could you? I was supposed to be your baby girl! Fuck you, fuck you, fuck you!" Toya screamed so loud she thought her lungs would explode. She brought the machete down on her father's face, neck, chest and shoulder. Blood collected on her face and naked body. She didn't stop swinging that machete until she was exhausted and her arms were aching. She dropped the big blade and fell onto her back in the pool of the blood that had formed around Moe. She lay there saturated in her old man's blood, breathing heavily, chest heaving up and down.

Chapter 15

Toya looked at her bloody hands and they were shaking crazily. She looked over at her father and he looked like something out of a *Hellraiser* movie. She suddenly felt nauseated and threw up beside him over and over again until she felt like her stomach was completely empty. Wiping her mouth with the back of her hand, she darted off down the hallway and turned the dials of the shower on. She sobbed uncontrollably, reliving what she'd done just minutes ago as she scrubbed her body with a soapy loofah. The hot shower water rinsed the blood from off her, turning it pink as it swirled down the drain. The medicine cabinet mirror was partially fogged by the time she stepped out of the tub and snatched a towel from off the rack. She was still sobbing and shaking while drying her hair and body. She wiped a circle in the medicine cabinet's mirror and looked at herself. She couldn't believe she'd killed someone. What was worse was that someone was her old man - her father. The thought brought great sorrow to her and she broke down again.

"No. No. No." Toya shook her head, with slimy ropes of snot hanging out of her nose. She looked up at her reflection at her glassy pink eyes and slick face. "I'm not gonna cry, I'm not gonna cry over some fuckin' monsta that beats and rapes me." She clenched her fists. She could literally hear Ramone saying those very words to her that night she'd crashed at his place. That's when it struck her to call him. There wasn't any way she could possibly get rid of her father's body by herself. She would need someone's help, and the only person she trusted to handle something like this was Ramone.

Toya blew her nose and cleaned herself up and washed her hands. She wrapped a towel around her and walked out of the bathroom. She snatched a blanket from out of the hallway closet and draped the blanket over her father's dead body. Next, she slipped on a bra, panties, and robe and picked up her cordless telephone. Holding the telephone, she noticed her hand was still trembling. She took the time to gather her wits, closing her eyes and taking a deep breath.

The telephone rang twice before Ramone picked up. "What up, li'l mama?"

"B-Bae, I-I need you to come over here, ASAP. I need you. I need your help," Toya admitted, wiping the excess wetness from her eyes.

"Yo, shorty, what happened?" Ramone asked, concerned.

"Baby, I really can't say over the phone. Just come over…" She gave him the address and hung up.

***

Toya sat on the couch, chain smoking cigarettes with mad thoughts running through her mind. Every five minutes she found herself peeking through the blinds to see if Ramone had arrived, but he'd yet to pull up. On top of that, she was paranoid as fuck! Every sound that night had her thinking it was the police snooping around, but that wasn't the case.

Toya, hearing a knock at the door, mashed out her cigarette and hopped to her feet. She stole a peek through the blinds and saw Ramone standing out on the front porch, keeping an eye on his surroundings. She unlocked the door as fast as she could to let him in. As soon as he locked the door behind him, she fell into his arms and sobbed into his chest. His brows crinkled and he wondered what was going on as he held her in his arms. He took in everything around him to see if anything was out of the ordinary. The only thing he made note of was the duffle bags and the guns on the dining room table.

That was enough to let him know that someone other than Toya was at the house.

"Shhhh. It's gonna be okay now, ma. Yo' nigga here now. Tell me what's up," Ramone told her, rubbing her back and kissing the top of her head.

Toya calmed down as best as she could and looked up at him. He wiped her eyes with the sleeve of his jacket while listening to what she had to say. As he took in the info, his face contracted with anger and he wished her father back to life just so he could smoke his old bitch ass again. "Where is he now?"

"In the bedroom. It's to your left, down the hall. You can't miss it."

Ramone kneeled down to the lump underneath the blanket. He was shocked when he pulled the blanket back and found Moe's butchered body underneath it. The sick, perverted fuck looked like Jason had gotten ahold of him.

So, this the slime ball that's been terrorizing my shorty all these years. Rest in shit, you ho-ass nigga, Ramone thought, crossing himself in the sign of the holy crucifix. *You lucky it was her and not me that laid claim to yo' worthless-ass life.*

"Arrrrrgh!" Ramone winced feeling Toya grasp his shoulder. He turned around, slipping his arm out of the sleeve of his jacket and then out of his shirt. She stood back with worry written across her face, wondering what was up.

"I'm sorry, baby. What did I do?" Toya asked, stepping closer to examine him. She saw blood absorbing the gauze lying over his shoulder. "Oh, my God, Ramone, what happened?"

"Ain't shit the god can't handle. This pain is kickin' my ass though," he told her. "I wish I had something to soothe my sufferin', nah mean?"

"Well, I've got some Ibuprofen in the medicine cabinet," she said. "I can go get it if you want."

"Nah. That nigga Jabari already gave me some, yo. I've been tossin' them shits back like popcorn and they aren't doin' jack shit." He winced. "You got something stronger?"

"Anything stronger like what?" Her brows wrinkled.

"I don't know, uh, coke, H?"

"Babe, you sure you wanna fuck with that stuff? I mean, I don't want chu to mess around and get addicted."

"Nah. That ain't gon' happen, shorty, believe me. Last thang a nigga wanna do is wind up all strung out like my Madukes and shit. You feel me?" she nodded understandingly. "So you holding or what?"

Toya dipped out of the bedroom and came back with the duffle bags her father had dropped on the dining room table. She sat them on the bed and unzipped them, one by one. Ramone's forehead wrinkled upon seeing all those Saran wrapped kilos.

"Damn, all this yo' OG's shit?" he asked, removing one of the kilos and whipping out his butterfly knife.

Yeah. He just re-upped. That's twenty keys right there." She pointed at the duffle bags. "Ten in each bag."

Ramone flipped open the butterfly knife, punctured the kilo, and pulled out some of the powdered substance. He tooted it up his nose and then he tooted a little more. He threw his head back, blinking his eyes, and snorted like a fat-ass hog. His eyes watered a little, but he blinked back the wetness.

"A'ight, baby, we're gonna have to dispose of Pops' body," Ramone told her after setting the kilo aside. He smacked the residue from the coke off his hands. "First things first, we're gonna have to…"

Ramone and Toya dragged Moe inside of the bathroom, stripped him naked, drained him of his blood, and chopped his big ass up. They wrapped up his severed body parts in black garbage bags and stored them inside of designer luggage. Ramone loaded up the bags inside the trunk of Moe's whip. He hopped in behind the wheel and fired it up.

Toya came running outside with enough stacks of blue-faced presidents to make a money phone. She passed it to Ramone and kissed him. He went back out of the backyard, but she held fast. When he looked back at her, she cupped his face and kissed him all over.

"I love you, Ramone. I truly do," a teary-eyed Toya confessed.

Ramone studied her eyes and saw truthfulness. It took a while, but he finally answered. "I love you too, shorty. From here on out, it's you and the kid. Word to everything I love."

Toya smiled happily and tears slid down her cheeks unevenly. Although she had fallen for Ramone really quick, it felt good and it felt right. She knew within her heart that he was the one.

"Does this mean I'm your girl now?"

"Hell nah." She looked away and he turned her to face him. "This means you're my queen and I'm your king, so never let anyone come between this union." He kissed her hand gently and then he kissed her long, deep and passionately. "Be ready when I get back," Ramone told her before backing out of the backyard and down the driveway. He adjusted his rearview mirror and saw Toya standing in the driveway. She blew him a kiss and waved goodbye. He grinned, cranked up the volume of the song Moe had been playing, and took off. Shortly, the backlights of the vehicle disappeared into the night.

Ramone drove out thirty-two minutes to the Bronx Zoo, where he bribed the zookeeper he knew. The old man used to trick off with his father's whores every Friday when he got his paycheck. He and Ramone garnered quite the relationship being that they were seeing each other so often. He'd give him and Jayshawn five bucks each to go to the store with. Sometimes he'd even let them steal pulls of his joint and swigs from his whiskey flask.

Ramone presented the zookeeper with the bread Toya had laid on him, and just like he figured, he accepted it. He didn't even bother to ask him the story behind the body parts. He figured the less he knew about the situation, the better, in case shit came back to bite him in the ass. The zookeeper killed the surveillance cameras, helped Ramone get the luggage out of the trunk, and over to the enclosure where the crocodiles were kept. After making sure the crocks had devoured every part of Moe's body, Ramone dapped up the zookeeper and got into the wind.

Chapter 16

Ramone cashed Moe's Camaro in at a chop shop and caught a taxi back to Toya's crib. She loaded all her personal belongings and the duffle bags into his whip and they drove back to the Red Hook Housing Projects. Ramone sat on the commode while Toya tended to the stitches of his wound.

"I can tell you know what you're doing," Ramone said, looking at her perform the task. "How many times have you done this?"

"More times than I can count," Toya replied, applying new dressing to his wound. "I'm the daughter of a street nigga. My daddy stayed in some shit that had me playing nurse."

The thought of what she'd done to her father hit her like the disciplining hand of a pimp. Her eyes became watery. She blinked and tears slid down her cheeks. Ramone frowned seeing her sorrowful eyes. She didn't have to tell him anything. He already knew what was affecting her.

"Don't you let another teardrop fall for that fuckin' monsta, ya hear me, ma? He doesn't deserve your tears of remorse. He doesn't deserve someone as sweet and as beautiful as you grieving over his sorry ass. Ya hear me?" Ramone told her, holding her chin upward and piercing into her eyes. They turned their heads at opposite angles and started kissing.

It was slow at first, but then the pace became intense and passionate. Their breathing was heavy and labored. They helped one another out of their clothes, snatched their bare feet out of their pants, and felt each other up. Their hands explored each other's bodies as the sounds of them making out filled the air.

Toya slipped her hand between them and grabbed his piece. She pumped it up and down, impressed by his girth and length. He expanded and lengthened in her small hand. The thick veins in his tool pulsated and clear gooey semen oozed out of its peehole. He forced her up against the sink, pumping into her grip while kissing her. Her nipples hardened and poked out. He slipped one of his fingers inside of her. Her treasure was warm and wet to his touch. He fingered her with his middle finger and rubbed on her rigid clit with his thumb. The feeling sent jolts of pleasure through her nether region. Her juices flowed out of her womb like water from an old, rusted, busted pipe. Her thick luscious legs trembled hard. Her eyes turned into slits, making her look like she was half Black and half Korean. She moaned and whined, feeling him suck on her bottom lip.

They kissed all the way inside of his bedroom, feeling each other up. Their eyes were closed and their breathing was heavy. Ramone pushed Toya back on the mattress, then picked up a butterfly knife and one of the kilos of coke. He busted that bitch open, took some onto his blade, and tooted it up his nose. He stood at the foot of the bed naked, watching Toya diddle her clit and suck on her nipples. Her moans were driving Ramone crazy. His dick got mad hard and its tip oozed a clear gel. He continued to indulge in the nose candy while she put on a performance worthy of a *Booty Talk* DVD.

Ramone kneeled down to Toya with some of the cocaine on his knife. He smiled delightedly as she tooted it up both of her nostrils and her eyes became glassy. He set his blade aside and sprinkled the coke over her exposed breasts and pussy. He slipped between her legs as she continued to please herself, snorting the powder off her chest and listening to her moan. Her essence spurted from between her thighs and her clitoris became rigid. When Ramone brought his head back up, cocaine residue fell from his nose and mouth. He kissed Toya deeply and roughly. He took a breast in each hand, mashed those beauties together, and devoured them. The sounds of him sucking and slurping on her made her squirt more and squirm around. She pressed her head back against the mattress and called out his name.

"Ramone, Ramone, Ramone, oooooooh!" Toya turned her head and bit into her arm. Her thighs shook madly and her pussy gushed. She purred like a kitten while tweaking her nipples and taking turns sucking them.

Ramone kissed down her flat stomach, snorting up some of the coke on his way down. Holding her thighs apart, he closed his eyes and pressed his face into her pussy. He inhaled her natural scent and it drove him insane. He kissed her inner thighs, then blew softly on her delicate flower. She started humping up into his face. She was horny as a bitch, and she wanted some dick right then.

"I want you to fuck me, baby! Fuck me like a savage! Show me who this pussy belongs to!" She placed his hand around her neck and told him to choke her.

Ramone squeezed her neck and she gagged. Her eyes welled up and she smiled freakily. She rubbed her clit in a circular motion, closing her eyes and licking her lips. He placed her leg on his shoulder and pushed the head of his pole against her opening. As soon as he sank inside of her warm, gooey center, her eyes rolled back and her mouth stayed open. She continued to manipulate her treasure. He held her thigh and cupped her left breast. He started stroking her faster and faster, going as far inside of her pink valley as he could. She whined and stimulated her jewel. Her mouth opened further and further. He threw his head back and squared his jaws. His hips became a blur, he was fucking her so hard and beastly.

"Uh, uh, uh, uh, right there! Yes, baby, right there! I-I feel it!" Toya cried out with a frown on her face. "I can-I can feel you in my stomach."

Ramone clutched her thigh and breast tighter. He growled, fucking her like a maniac. He became hot and sticky. Sweat peppered his face and the rest of his body. He breathed heavily as he gave her little ass the business. Her sexual cries turned him on, making his piece stronger and harder.

"Ooooooh, shit, baby, here I cum! Here I fuckin' cum! Ooooh, godddd!" Toya screamed and jerked violently, then went stiff. Her coochie spurted and sprayed. It was almost like she was taking a piss. She lay on her back, eyes closed, spanking her bald monkey. Jolts of pleasure shot up and down her lower region. She had another orgasm and then another until she started shaking again.

Ramone removed her hand from her pussy, placed her other leg on his shoulder, and pressed his fists on either side of her body. He slammed his tool home and she yelped, nearly jumping out of her skin. Grunting, he began stroking her tight, little kitten with no remorse, making her make the ugliest sex faces he'd ever seen in his sixteen years of living. He gave her every inch he had, hitting the bottom of that mothafucking thang. It sounded like someone's grandmomma was stirring up a pot of macaroni and cheese.

"Uh, uh, uh, o-o-ooh, yes! That's it, give it to me, baby! Give it to meeeeeeee!" she belted like Anita Baker in concert in front of a sold out crowd. Her body bounced up and down as he slammed into her recklessly. His arm muscles, buttocks, and calves flexed. Sweat poured down his face, down his back, and vanished into the crack of his ass.

"Ahhh, shit! I'm 'bouta, I'm 'bouta nut," Ramone stammered, holding her gaze. She flicked her tongue at him, enticing him.

"Gimme that nut, daddy, this yo' pussy! Splash all up in me," Toya prompted him with a low, sensual tone, making his pipe tingle. She clenched and unclenched her pussy's muscle, driving him wild. Her twat became wetter and hotter. He balled her up and started pummeling her shit. His sweat peppered her face. She narrowed her eyes, whining louder and louder.

"Here I cum, ma! Here I cum!" Ramone hollered, pumping and grinding inside of her womb. He went to pull out, but she locked her legs around his waist. He bucked as he splashed his gooey children inside of her. She grumbled and came right behind him, shaking like crazy. He fell on top of her and she wrapped her arms around him. She kissed the side of his face while rubbing him up and down his back lovingly.

"That was good, baby," Toya said, staring up at the ceiling.

"You ain't never lied, shorty," Ramone replied. She turned him to her and they kissed.

The kissing made Ramone's soldier stand at attention and he was ready to get it popping again. He straddled Toya, grabbed a handful of her hair, and stuffed her mouth with his meat. Her mouth was as wet as rain and as hot as an oven on 450°. She looked him straight in his eyes as he fucked her mouth. She gagged loudly and spilled thick bubbly ropes of saliva down her chin. The sound of her choking on the end of his pole turned him on. He started pumping between her lips harder and faster. Her eyes became teary. She held his butt cheeks, trying to force him further down her throat. Still holding her by her hair, he leaned backwards, fingering her twat and rubbing her clit. He looked at her like he couldn't stand her ass, gritting his teeth and steadily humping her mouth. Her eyes fluttered and she came again while massaging his nutsack.

She suddenly fell back on the bed, holding her pussy and crossing her legs. She bit down on her bottom lip as she shook like she was having a seizure. Ramone jumped up and stood over her. He held one hand at his side while using the other to pump his shit.

"Hmmmmmmmph," Ramone said blissfully as he relieved himself. His dick head swelled and then his warm, gel-like semen squirted out of his peehole. It came out in small ropes and then it rained down on Toya, pelting her breasts. She smiled up at him with satisfaction while rubbing her titties. He kneeled down beside her and kissed her in the mouth. He didn't give a fuck that she'd just finished sucking his dick. As far as he was concerned, his swipe was clean and she was his little baby.

Ramone rested for like thirty minutes, flipped Toya on her stomach, and knocked her legs apart with his knee. He rammed his dick in her all the way down to the hilt, held her head down into the mattress, and fucked her like Buns fucked Kisha in *Belly*. Once he'd put that ass to sleep, he covered her with a blanket and kissed her on the side of her head.

Ramone threw on a pair of sweatpants, then picked up his piece and the kilo they'd been indulging in earlier. He carried everything into the living room, where he plopped down on the raggedy couch. He broke off half of the kilo, smoothed out the clumps in it, and prepared three lines of it. Using a rolled-up one dollar bill, he tooted two lines up his nose and fell back on the couch. He stared up at the ceiling while the coke took its course. His eyes turned glassy and he pulled on his nose. A feeling of euphoria came over him as the drug manipulated his mind.

Ramone had fallen into a deep, dark depression after Jayshawn had been murdered. He tried his best to keep himself together, but he found it difficult to function when he was sober.

"Damn, bro, this one really hurt, yo!" Ramone's eyes pooled with tears and slid down his cheeks. He wiped his face with the back of his hand and sniffled. "It's like since you've been gone, I've been feeling this great, big void inside of me. And no matter what a nigga do to try to fill it, it stays empty."

Ramone tooted up the last line from the coffee table and dug in his nose. Seeing a distorted image at the corner of his eye, he snatched up his pole and pointed it in that direction. The distorted image was Jayshawn! Ramone blinked his eyes several times, but the image wouldn't come into focus.

"Bro, that's you? I thought-I thought you were d-dead." Ramone lowered his pole as his brother approached him. When he finally came into focus, he was wearing a smile and opening his arms for a hug. Ramone shed tears of joy and a smile spread across his lips. He ran into his brother's arms and he hugged him. Jayshawn held him in his arms listening to him sob into his chest and kissing him on top of his head. "I missed you, bro. I missed you so much. I don't ever wanna be without you."

"I've missed you too, kid. Word is bond," Jayshawn replied, holding him at arm's length. "Look here, I know you hurting and you'd much rather be dead, but shorty, you're still young. You've gotta whollllle lot more living to do. On top of that, you owe me a body."

"I owe you a body?" Ramone frowned.

Jayshawn looked him in the eyes with a serious expression. "Yeah, baby boy, you owe me a body, and I can't rest 'til that debt is collected."

Ramone understood then what he was getting at. He wanted the nigga that peeled his cap dead. "You gon' get'cho body, bro. I swear to God, you got that coming."

"Babe, who're you talking to?" Toya asked groggily from the bedroom door, holding the sheet over her nakedness.

Ramone snapped back to reality, blinking his eyes like he didn't know where he was. He then made a 360 degree turn, looking around for Jayshawn. It was like he had never even been there! He took a deep breath and slid his hands down his face.

Either that shit was real, or it's the coke that's fucking with me. "No one, shorty, just thinking out loud," Ramone replied.

Toya yawned and stretched her right arm. "Well, come back to bed. I can't sleep without you. You know how I like to cuddle."

"A'ight. I'll be right there."

"Okay. Don't keep me waiting." Toya turned around and walked back inside the bedroom.

Ramone gathered up everything he'd brought into the living room, walked back inside his bedroom, and shut the door behind him.

Chapter 17

Ramone and Toya were laid up at the crib when Jabari hit him up. Ramone started to ignore his call, but Toya convinced him to do otherwise. Jabari was trying to get Ramone to come out with him and the homies to the strip club. He was dedicated to getting the young nigga's mind off of his brother for the time being. Ramone gave him every excuse in the book to avoid going, but seeing her man really needed to get out of the house, Toya snatched his cell phone and told Jabari he'd be down in thirty minutes. Ramone didn't put up much of a fight because he knew his lady was right. He took care of his hygiene, got dressed, and concealed his heat in his waistband. He kissed Toya goodbye and headed down stairs. Now here the young shooter-in-training was, riding in the backseat of Jibbs' whip taking in the scenery of the grimy streets of east Harlem.

"Yo, Dunn, the hoes at this new strip joint better be fine or I'ma be pissed," Jibbs said from behind the wheel. His eyes were low and his speech was slurred thanks to the Dirty Sprite he'd been consuming. He was a nineteen-year-old dark-skinned nigga who rocked a mouthful of gold. His wild hair and mouth full of gold made him look like one of them Jacksonville niggas. His left eye was lazy and twitched every time he was heated.

"Blood, stop tryna act like you got standards. I done seen you fuck on dopefiends," Jabari reminded him from the passenger seat, where he watched the streets from his window.

Everyone inside of the car busted up laughing except for Ramone. He had a face of stone.

"Fuck y'all niggas, bruh. Pussy don't got no face," Jibbs replied.

"Only niggas that'll smash anything think like that, son."

111

Spank laughed, clapping his hands. He was a chubby light-skinned dude, twenty-two in age with a baby face. He had a dollar sign inked at the corner of his right eye and his neck and arms were tattooed as well.

"You ain't never lied, son," Jibbs spoke up with Spank over his shoulder.

"Yo, you good, my nigga? You've been mad quiet back here." Spank nudged Ramone.

"Yeah, I'm Gucci. Just thinking is all," Ramone replied.

"About what?" Spank pried.

"About all the pussy we're about to see, you nosy fuck," Jabari interjected, spying on Spank through the sun-visor mirror. "Lay off my li'l nigga. He'll be a'ight. Especially once he gets all this ass and pussy thrown in his face. Ain't that right, King?"

"Fa sho," Ramone said with a weak smile. His eyes were glassy and he was drowning in thoughts of his brother. He wanted to break down, but refrained from fear of being looked at as soft.

"That's my guy." Jabari grinned.

Jibbs pulled up at a red traffic light. Seeing swift movement at the corner of his eye, he grabbed his piece where it was wedged between the seat and armrest and pointed at the driver's side window. A shabbily-dressed man with a scruffy, graying beard jumped back and threw up his hands. His eyes widened and his mouth stretched open.

"Say, bruh, I nearly blew yo' shit back. Fuck you want, nigga?" Jibbs spat, lazy eye twitching eerily. He was pissed off because the old dopefiend had blown his high.

"Black Man, I'm just-I'm just tryna make a couple of dollars. Lemme clean ya windows fa ya," the old dopefiend said.

Jibbs and Jabari could tell the old nigga was dope sick.

"Fuck naw, man! I don't need you fuckin' up my windows

and shit," Jibbs retorted, throwing his head to the back. "Now get the hell on before I-"

"Relax, nigga." Jabari grabbed him by his arm.

"What'chu mean relax?" Jibbs frowned.

"Just like I said, nigga, relax. You can't see the desperation in an old head's eyes?" Jabari asked.

"Yeah, I see it. And I don't give a shit what he's going through, tough luck."

"Have a heart, nigga. With all the dust we kickin' up in these streets, it's only right we look out for the less fortunate from time to time to keep ourselves in God's good graces," Jabari told him. "Yo, OG, keep it a hunnit with me. What'chu gon' use the bread for I'ma give you for cleaning the homie's windows?"

"Yo, son, the light is green," Spank told Jabari, pointing at the traffic light.

"Nigga, fuck that light!" Jabari replied, keeping his eyes on the fiend. "Like I was saying, OG, what would you do with that bread?"

The old dopefiend stared at Jabari like he was weighing his options of what he should tell him. He could lie and get the money. Or he could tell the truth and end up not getting shit. He knew he was taking the risk of not getting anything, but he decided to trust his instincts. Taking a deep breath, he went on to tell Jabari what he'd planned to do with the money he'd earn cleaning his windows. "A'ight, you said keep it a hunnit, so that's exactly what I'ma do. Fuck it! I plan on taking whatever you gon' bless me with and putting it towards my next high. I'm jonesin' and needa get right. My old ass is ill, son. I'm talking mad ill." He put his hand to his stomach. Everyone peeped the stains on his clothes. Old head had been throwing up from the lack of dope in his system.

"What's got the streets talking up here, my G? What they fuckin' with?" Jabari inquired.

"Heroin, but not just any heroin. Rebirth. It's got the streets goin' bonkers."

A surprised look came across Jabari's face upon hearing the name of the dope. It was the same shit Sanka was talking about. This information most definitely garnered his attention. He had Jibbs pull over so he could pick the old dopefiend's mind while he tended to the windows. He found out that there were several houses throughout the eastside of Harlem. They were all run by Dominicans, and they were pulling in mad loot pumping Rebirth. The old head said Rebirth had turned east Harlem into *The Night of the Living Dead*. Dopefiends were staggering around like zombies and shit.

"Hmm," Jabari said as the gears began to turn inside his head. He stared out the corners of his eyes and massaged his chin. Spank and Jibbs peeped the look etched across their big homie's face. They could tell he had a bright idea, and his bright ideas usually meant them getting into some trouble, or getting to some money - both of which they wanted plenty of.

"Yo, my man, you tryna make a few dollars?" Jabari asked the old dopefiend, holding up a small wad of twenty dollar bills.

The old head's eyes bulged like they were about to pop out of his head. He licked his big, chapped lips and rubbed his calloused hands together greedily. All he could think about was how much Rebirth he could buy with the money. "Helllll yeah, just tell a nigga what he gotta do and it's done. Ya heard?" the old dopefiend replied excitedly.

"Well, step inside of my office. Open the back door, Spank," Jabari told one of the shooters from over his shoulder. As soon as Spank opened the back door, he and Ramone were smacked across the face with an overwhelming odor. The old head smelled like a combination of ass, musty dick, and sweaty gym socks. Spank and Ramone frowned up and covered their nose and mouth.

"Goddamn, this nigga funky denna muthafucka!" Spank said.

"Mannn, scoot cho ass over so this nigga can get in," Jabari spat.

Spank did like he was told, bitching the entire time. The old dopefiend slid into the backseat and slammed the door shut. Jabari gave the driver the hand signal and he drove away.

"Yo, bruh, on some real shit, you gotta crack a window in this bitch or something," Ramone protested. "Niggas can only hold their breath for so long, word to Jayshawn."

Jibbs rolled down the windows and let some fresh air inside.

Jabari promised to hit the old dopefiend's hand with two hundred dollars after he took him to the trap houses he knew about in Spanish Harlem. He planned to hit all them shits! He knew that nigga Sanka would feel it in his pockets, but he didn't give a rat's ass. His African ass had insulted him by handling him like a bitch, and he wasn't about to let it slide. He had a reputation to live up to.

Jabari, Jibbs, Spank, and Ramone drove back to the Murder Quarters. They got vested up and bangered down, snatched an Astro van, and went out on their mission. They were going to hit all of Sanka's spots that the old dopefiend could remember. Payback was a bitter, trifling-ass baby mama!

***

Akachukwu had to be one of the luckiest sons of bitches to have ever been pushed from between a woman's legs. The brutal stabbing from Hoffa's top goon had him teetering between life and death. The medical staff was able to salvage him, but he'd lost a hell of a lot of blood. Fortunately for him, they had some Universal Blood on deck in the infirmary. Otherwise he'd be up in the clouds trying to negotiate his way into Heaven.

Though Akachukwu had gotten a second chance at life, he was still in a great deal of pain. The lead nurse provided him with a morphine drip to ease his suffering. The painkiller had him in LaLa Land and he drifted off to sleep smiling. His smile turned into a frown as he awoke in a snake pit. He could literally feel the serpents slip around his wrists and ankles. He struggled to pull free of them, but he couldn't break their hold. The next thing he knew, one of them clamped down around his mouth and his eyes popped open. He realized he was in the infirmary with Scorpion standing over him, holding his hand over his mouth. What he thought were snakes wrapping around his wrists and ankles were actually tourniquets.

Akachukwu looked back up at Scorpion fearfully. His eyes were terrifying and he was wearing an evil smile. Scorpion looked around the room to make sure no one was spying on him. Most of the beds were empty, and the patients that were there were asleep. Scorpion leaned down to Akachukwu so only he could hear what he had to say.

"Hey there, sunshine, it looks like I'll be going home soon," Scorpion told him. "I couldn't leave without saying goodbye. This is from Hoffa, Blood." His face balled up hatefully and he presented an eight-inch shank.

Akachukwu bucked against his restraints in bed, but he couldn't get away. Scorpion jabbed him in the heart twenty-five times until his body went rigid. For good measure, he stabbed him one last time in the chest, leaving the fashioned knife standing up in his chest. Akachukwu's eyes were wide and his mouth was hanging open. The blood from his wounds saturated his gown quickly.

Scorpion took the time to admire his handiwork before walking away. He vanished within the shadowy area of the infirmary. The medical staff walked back and forth across the patients' rooms, attending to different tasks. They were oblivious to the fact that one of the people that was in their care had just been murdered.

Chapter 18

Two Dominican men wearing latex gloves sat at the kitchen table packaging heroin into packets stamped "Rebirth" and placing them aside in neat piles. There were a number of items on the tabletop, including three guns, two kilos of the dope, and several Rebirth stamped packets. Every now and again, the men would wipe the sweat from their brows and take a swig of their Presidentes (a very popular beer in the Dominican Republic).

"Por qué ustedes dos hijos de puta no se mueven y vienen a ayudarnos con esta mierda? (Why don't you two mothafuckas get off your asses and come help us with this shit?)" Poncho spat at the other two Dominican men, who were playing Madden on the 50-inch flat screen television set. They were joking, laughing, and talking shit to each other over their game. They were loud and boisterous, behaving like a couple of college roommates.

"Eso es lo que estoy diciendo! Trabaja ahora, juega más tarde! (That's what I'm saying! Work now, play later!)" Tito said angrily, snatching off his snapback and throwing it across the room. It hit one of the Dominican men in the head. Keeping his eyes on the television's screen, he laughed and threw up the middle finger.

"Relax. I'm blowing this fool out. We'll be done in a second," Alberto responded. He was giving Chicho, the one that had gotten the snapback thrown at him, that work.

"On some real shit, my nigga, if y'all don't pause that shit and come help with this, I'ma take this butcher knife——" he held up the butcher's knife he'd used it to open up one of the kilos of Rebirth on the table top."——and slice those fuckin' cords, then nobody will be playing jack shit. Comprende, homeboy?"

"Whatever, tough guy, we're almost finished." Alberto retorted, waving him off, obviously not taking him seriously.

Tito looked from Poncho to Alberto. He didn't like being brushed off like he wasn't to be concerned about, so he was going to make good on his threat. Jumping to his feet with the butcher knife, he marched into the living room, stealing everyone's attention. He'd gotten halfway across the living room when what felt like a meteorite burst through the door, and splinters flew in every direction. The Dominicans' heads snapped towards the front door, where they saw Jabari, Jibbs, Spank, and Ramone. They were rocking red ski masks and toting bangers.

"Bet' not one muthafucka in here move, or——"

Jibbs' warning was cut short when Poncho snatched his pole from the table. He was far too late on the draw. Spank and Ramone upped their silenced guns and unloaded on that ass. Poncho flipped over the kitchen table and brought it down along with him. The kilos, empty packets, packets of dope, and bottles of beer fell to the floor chaotically. Poncho lay on his back wearing the dead look. His blood poured from his wounds and turned the heroin into a red pasty substance.

Seeing the intruders occupied with Poncho, Chicho decided it was the best time to make his move. He locked eyes with Tito, letting him know he was about to go for it. Tito shook his head no. Chicho mouthed to him, "Fuck that! I'm not going out like that." Chicho reached for his pole. Jabari peeped the desperate attempt, upped his shotgun, and obliterated his dome. It looked like chunks of raw hamburger meat and spaghetti sauce splattered on the coffee table and carpet.

"Estúpido mierda! (you stupid fuck!)" Tito shook his head, thinking of how foolish Chicho was to make such a move when the odds were stacked against them. He dropped the butcher knife at his feet, crossed himself in the sign of the holy crucifix and lifted his hands up. Alberto followed suit, lifting his hands up. This was letting Jabari and them know he didn't want any trouble.

"Y'all niggas get whatever dope that doesn't have that dead nigga's blood on it," Jabari ordered Spank and Ramone. The savages tucked their guns, whipped out black garbage bags and rushed to do Jabari's bidding.

Jabari hoisted his shotgun over his shoulder, smacked Alberto across the back of his head, and ordered him to stand up beside Tito. He complied.

"Now I know y'all gotta be holding more than that, so where's the rest of the shit?" Jabari asked.

"Bro, you have no idea whose operation you're fucking with! Once Sanka finds out about——"

Tito was abruptly cut short by a kick in the balls. As soon as he doubled over, Jabari rewarded him with a backhanded punch. He flew off his feet and crashed into the flat screen television. Sparks flew out of the TV and it wafted with smoke.

Jibbs turned to Poncho, who was staring at the floor with his eyes closed, praying to God in Spanish while clutching a rosary in his hand. Using his banger, Jibbs knocked the baseball cap from off his crown of curly hair and lifted his chin so he'd be looking him directly in the eyes.

"My man, you already know what it is. My nigga over here is not gonna repeat himself," Jibbs warned him, with a devilish look in his eyes. Poncho knew for sure that the Brooklyn Demon wouldn't hesitate to splash him, so he gave up the whereabouts of the safe and its combination.

Jabari smiled wickedly behind his ski mask. He patted Poncho on his cheek like he was a Made Man in the mafia and Poncho was an underling. He then told his demons to hold it down and went to retrieve the goods he'd been told about.

Jabari and his demons fled the house and disappeared into the darkness. They left Poncho lying on his side in the bedroom with his mouth gagged and his wrists bound behind his back. He screamed and squirmed, trying to get free.

***

Three Dominican men lay on their stomachs with their mouths gagged and their wrists bound behind their back. A fourth one lay slumped in a chair at the kitchen table with his legs outstretched before him. His eyes were bucked, his mouth was open, and his arms were hanging lifelessly at his sides. His gun's trigger guard hung loosely from his finger. He'd managed to get off a shot when Jabari and his demons crashed their spot. It was just too bad that for that one bullet he sent at them, they sent ten times more at him.

Spank and Jabari were at the kitchen table where the Dominicans had been packaging the Rebirth for distribution. They swept the packets of the potent dope and whatever kilos were on the table into their black garbage bags while Ramone stood guard over the Dominican niggas. Holding his gun at his side, Ramone stared them down as they mugged him. He could tell by the look in their eyes if they could get their hands on a banger, they'd soak him and the homies' asses up.

Look at these muthafuckas, yo. These Spanish niggas so mad they turning red in the face, Ramone thought, clenching and unclenching his jaws. His eyes twinkled hatefully. It was some Dominicans that had been selling dope to his moms during most of her stint as a dopefiend. In fact, that shooting gallery he'd found her in belonged to some east Harlem niggas that he was sure had been pumping that poison into the ghetto. As far as he was concerned, they were responsible for his moms walking around like a fucking zombie. At least, that's

122

what he was telling himself right then. Shit, the young nigga was hurting inside and he needed somebody to take his pain and suffering out on.

Scrunching his face, he hawked up a big, slimy ball of mucus and spat on the face of the Dominican he assumed was running the spot. He was a medium-built man of a cinnamon-brown complexion. He rocked a goatee, a blue bandana around his cornrows, and a light-blue denim Dickie shirt. The love of his life, Elmira, was inked on the side of his neck, big, bold and fancy-like.

The medium-built Dominican man went by the name Adalfo. He wiped his face off on the carpet as best as he could, but he still had some yellowish goo hanging from his nose. He looked up at Jabari hatefully with a vein swelling at the center of his forehead. His eyes turned glassy and red webs formed on them. He said some shit in Spanish that Ramone didn't understand, given his mouth was gagged and he couldn't speak properly.

"Yo, we got all they shit. That's it, B!" Spank told Jabari, holding up the black garbage bag of goods.

"This a pretty good take we've got for the night," Jabari told Spank, holding out his fist.

"Hell yeah. Niggas gon' eat good. That's for damn sure." Spank dapped him up.

"Come on, King, let's roll," Jabari said, hoisting his shotgun over his shoulder and making his way towards the door. He'd gotten halfway there when Ramone called him back, halting him in his tracks.

"Yeah. You right, boss dog, this is a nice li'l take, but I bet'cha there's more," Ramone told him while holding Adalfo's mean mug stare. "And this arroz blanco and lechon asado-eating bitch knows where it is."

"More?" Spank's forehead wrinkled. He looked at Jabari, who was massaging his chin thinking on the situation.

"Yeah. I want more, and Mr. Get Bad here is gonna tell me exactly where it is. Ain't that right, homeboy?" Ramone asked Adalfo, thumping his forehead and making him wince. He pulled the gag out of Adalfo's mouth to hear his reply.

I'm not telling you jack shit, muthafucka! Not one muthafuckin' thang," Adalfo swore. "That's on my dead homies, Rest in Peace."

"Oh, yeah? Well, we'll see about that," Ramone told him. He then looked over at Jabari for the okay. He gave him the nod, which made him smile wickedly. Ramone tucked his banger and rubbed his hands together. "I'm 'bouta show yo' monkey-ass how a reallllll Brooklyn Demon gets down. Word is bond." He addressed Jabari and Spank. "Yo, y'all snatch his bitch-ass up, strap 'em down on the kitchen table, and pull his pants down around his ankles. The kid got something for his ass - literally."

Chapter 19

Upon hearing Ramone's commands, Adalfo hollered and squirmed to get free from his bonds. Spank stepped up and kicked him in his mouth, bloodying his grill. Ramone ducked off inside of the bedroom, flipping on the light switch and riffling inside of the closet. While he was in there doing whatever, Spank and Jabari did exactly like he said. A couple of minutes later, Ramone returned, untangling the neck of a wire hanger. Once he'd gotten the hanger to its full length, he motioned for Spank and Jabari to step aside so he'd have room to practice. They obliged his request and watched him in action.

Ramone threw the hanger over his shoulder and cast it forward like it was a whip. It whistled as it sliced through the air. Adalfo looked over his shoulder, wide-eyed and nervous. His heart raced upon seeing Ramone practicing with the hanger. He had yet to be struck with it, but he could already imagine how it would feel against his buttocks.

"Yo, man, what the-what the fuck you plan on doin' with that?" Adalfo asked, voice trembling.

"You're about to find out inna sec, my nigga. Don't even trip." Jabari smiled from behind the ski mask before smacking him across his ass, making him buck. He left a red hand impression behind and a stinging sensation behind.

"Now you gon' either tell us where some more dope is stashed, or where yo' people stash houses at? If not, I'm 'bouta paint so many stripes on yo' ass niggas 'round here gon' swear yo' Mexican ass a zebra."

"Aye, I'm Dominican!" Adalfo corrected him.

"Dominican, Sminican, nigga, all y'all talk the same talk and eat the same shit! Now tell me and my niggas what the fuck we wanna know!" Ramone demanded, striking him across his back with the hanger. Adalfo hollered like a wounded animal, scrunching his face, and balling his fists. As if by magic, a reddish-purple bruise formed across his back.

"I'm not tellin' you ass jack shit, bro! You're gonna have to kill me, first!" Adalfo told him between winces.

Ramone shook his head and blinked his eyes. He slid his hand down his face and took a closer look at the brazen Dominican. It wasn't Adalfo staring back at him, but Paperchase.

"You hear me, muthafucka? You're gonna have to kill me and send me where yo' punk-ass brother is!" he taunted, laughing like a psycho maniac.

Clenching his jaws, Ramone mugged him hard. Adalfo's face interchanged with Paperchase's. The sadistic mothafucka continued to laugh, making a mockery of him. The young nigga clenched his jaws tighter and the hanger in his hand. Angry, he trembled all over and then exploded like a powder keg.

"Fuck youuuuuu!" Ramone bellowed, swinging the hanger down with full force.

Whoooooosh! Whaaackkk!

The hanger licked Adalfo's buttocks, making him buck and holler. Spank and the other Dominicans lying gagged and bound in the living room cringed. They felt their comrade's pain. It was like they were the ones being assaulted.

Jabari saw that things were about to get loud and messy so he picked up the remote control to the flat screen mounted on the wall. He changed the channel to some BET movie and cranked the volume up dumb high, then tossed the remote aside.

"You think shit sweet downtown, yo? Well, I'm 'bouta show you, son! Word to the borough!" Ramone shouted with madness twinkling in his eyes. All he could see was Paperchase in agony, and his suffering brought him great pleasure knowing how he'd murdered his brother, Jayshawn.

Whack, whaackk, whaaackkk, whaaaackkkk!

The hanger came down fast and furiously, showing no mercy. Lick after lick caused bloody welts to appear on Adalfo's back and buttocks. Everyone watching cringed and looked away, except for Jabari. He smiled like a proud father watching his son take his first steps. He said he was going to turn the young'un into a demon, and he was taking form right before his eyes.

Whack, whaackk, whaaackkk, whaaaackkkk!

"Oh, bitch-ass nigga, I'ma show you what time it is, fucking with a young nigga like me!" Ramone swore, bringing the hanger down harder against his victim's nakedness. Adalfo's cries and screams excited him to no end. He enjoyed making his brother's murderer pay for his sins.

Ramone snatched off his ski mask and exposed his sweaty face. He looked like he'd completely lost it. He ignored Adalfo's pleas to stop. He kept punishing him, painting stripes on his ass like he promised. Dots of blood clung to Ramone's face, and more and more of it collected on top of what was already there. He didn't care though. He kept beating on Adalfo who he imagined was Paperchase.

"Fuck you crying for, bitch? Huh? If you would have never taken my brother, this would have never even fuckin' happened! This is all yo' fucking fault, you hear me? Huh?"

Whack, whaackk, whaaackkk! Whaaaackkkk!

Ramone's shadow cast on the wall, displaying his savage attack on Adalfo. Dots of blood collected on the door of the oven, counter, and floor. The Dominicans on the living room floor looked away. They could no longer stand to see Ramone pulverizing their comrade. That nigga Spank couldn't take it any more either. He turned his back on the horror show.

Ramone had completely zoned out. He was so caught up in the moment that he'd blocked out all sound. He couldn't hear Jabari at his back ordering him to stop. It wasn't until he grabbed him from behind, snatched the hanger from out of his hand, and gave him a backhand smack that he snapped back to reality. Gasping, Ramone looked around like he didn't know where he was. He looked to the Dominicans gagged and bound on the floor, Spank who was looking at him like he'd lost his mind, Adalfo lying on top of the table barely conscious with his back looking like Jesus' in *The Passion of the Christ*, and then finally to the door of the microwave, where he saw his reflection staring back at him. The young'un looked wild as shit with his messy dreadlocks and mixture of blood and sweat on his face.

"Yo, king, you didn't have to go that far. The nigga already had given in," Jabari told him. "He managed to say he didn't know where any more dope was, but he knew where some money was at. I just hope you haven't sent 'em to that big ghetto in the sky before he was able to come up off that info." Ramone didn't say a word. He was fixated on the wire hanger in Jabari's fist. It was dripping blood on the kitchen floor. "Yo, my G, you good?" he asked, tossing the bloody hanger aside and grasping his shoulder. He looked him right in his eyes.

Hesitantly, Ramone nodded yes and swallowed spit. He turned on the faucet and rinsed the blood off his face. He snatched a couple of paper towels down, and patted his face dry. When he turned around, he saw Jabari kneeled in front of Adalfo with a fistful of his hair. He had the battered and bleeding man's head turned sideways so he could see his face while he was talking to him.

"I know-I know the-the route that his-his carriers take to pick up the money he's collected for the week pumpin' dope," Adalfo wheezed weakly with his eyes narrowed into slits. "Me and-me and my soldados planned on hittin'-hittin' 'em for-for everything."

"Oh, yeah? Well, how much is everything?"

"I-I don't know I…aaah!" Adalfo winced and screamed from Jabari yanking his head back.

"Cut the shit! I know you know." Jabari mugged him.

"No-no. I swear on the Virgin Mary I don't have any idea, but it has to be a lot."

"What makes you say that?"

"This-this Rebirth shit, man. It's the-it's the best dope to have ever hit the market," Adalfo stressed. "This shit has the streets goin' bananas, my nigga. Niggas up here been makin' more dough then we know what to do with."

Jabari nodded. He knew Adalfo wasn't lying because the old dopefiend had told him same shit. "A'ight, gimme the route and the time they usually leave to make the pickups."

Jabari listened intently to what Adalfo told him, storing all the data inside his mind. He pulled open a few of the drawers until he came across one with silverware in it. He removed a butcher knife and held it to his face. He could see his reflection in it. Jabari walked up to Ramone and handed him the butcher knife with its blade. The young nigga took the knife, looking at it and then up at Jabari like he didn't know what he wanted him to do with it.

"You started it, so finish it, King," Jabari told him, seemingly reading his mind. He nodded to Adalfo and then to the two Dominicans gagged and bound in the living room. "Is there a problem?" he asked with a raised eyebrow.

"Fuck naw. Tonight's these fools' last night on earth," Ramone replied with a scrunched up face, looking like a demon in the flesh. He flipped the knife over in his hand so he'd be holding it by its handle.

Jabari grinned happily, grabbed him by the back of his head, and pressed his forehead against his. He held it there for a moment while staring into his eyes. "You're my proudest creation." Holding Ramone by both sides of his face, he kissed him on his forehead like he was his child or some shit. "We'll be waiting outside, son." He patted him on his shoulder and walked away, signaling for Spank to follow him. As soon as the homies had left, Ramone pulled his ski mask back down over his face and approached Adalfo. He was so weakened from the beating that all he could do was lay there and wait for the younger man to end his life. Ramone, without remorse, pulled Adalfo's head back by his hair and slit his throat.

Adalfo's neck erupted in blood, pouring out until it began to drip. He twitched uncontrollably for a while before becoming rigid. With him out of the way, Ramone set his sights on the Dominicans in the living room. Their eyes bucked, they hollered into their gags, and squirmed, seeing him stalk towards them.

Chapter 20

Three minutes later, Ramone walked out of the house, pulling the front door closed behind him. He pulled his hood over his head, stuck his hands in his pockets, and walked out of the front yard. The way he was carrying himself, anyone watching would have sworn he'd just left from visiting relatives instead of having departed from three killing mothafuckas.

Ramone hopped into the van and it quickly peeled off. He stared up at the ceiling listening to Spank and them talk about what he'd done back at the house. They spoke about him like he wasn't even there, and truthfully he wasn't for sure if he was, because no one could possibly convince him that it had been him that had just murdered those three men in cold blood.

"Yeah, son, that young nigga's a real life demon," Spank said.

"Oh yeah?" Jibbs replied.

"Word is bond."

***

Jabari and his demons tailed a triple-black, big body Chevrolet Suburban with pitch-black tinted windows and bulletproof exterior. The way that bitch looked, niggas would have sworn a politician or someone was riding in it, but that wasn't the case. There were a total of three people onboard the truck: two gung-ho shooters Sanka had picked himself specifically for this assignment, and Sankeesy. Come to find out, Sanka didn't trust a soul with his money, so he never let anyone conduct this aspect of his business alone. Sankeesy was family, so he felt comfortable having her ride along with his muscle to make the pickups. Not only was little mama his cousin, she was one of the only people he trusted.

Jabari counted at least six duffle bags the shooters and Sankeesy had picked up along their route. The duffle bags were so loaded that the two shooters had trouble carrying them out to the truck by themselves. Jabari couldn't stop smiling when he saw this because he knew they were looking at one hell of a payday once they got their hands on them.

Jabari and his demons found themselves in a real seedy part of Harlem none of them were familiar with. They parked four cars back from the Chevy Suburban, slumped down in their seats, and watched the shooters hop out of the truck. The shooters scanned their surroundings for any threats. Once they were sure the perimeter was clear, one stood guard while the other helped Sankeesy out of the vehicle.

The shooters walked towards the stash house with Sankeesy secured between them. When they reached the front door of the spot, Sankeesy knocked on the door in a secret code that let whoever was on the inside know that it was her coming to pick up the money. After she was identified through the eye slot, a series of locks were undone and the front door opened. Once the shooters and Sankeesy were let inside of the stash house, Jabari and his savages pulled their ski masks over their faces and readied their guns. Jibbs and Spank were the first to hop out of the van. Under the cover of night, they hunched over and made their way to the back of the stash house. Jibbs contacted Jabari through his earbud to let him know they'd taken their post at the back of the house. Jabari and Ramone jumped out of the van and closed the door back quietly. The old dopefiend sat behind the wheel, scratching the inside of his track marked arm. He watched Jabari and Ramone strategically make their way inside of the yard and camouflage themselves inside of the bushes.

The shooters and Sankeesy emerged from the stash house. They came down the steps as the front door was shut and locked behind them. They'd gotten halfway across the yard when they heard rustling within the bushes. The shooter closest to Sankeesy pulled her behind him to shield her from the possible threat of gunfire. He and his comrade then unzipped their duffle bags and pulled out Tec-9s. Before they could have the chance to finger fuck their triggers, Jabari and Ramone sprung from the bushes, lighting their asses up. The shooters wore masks of agony as they fell backwards with bodies riddled with holes. They collided with the ground and cash went up into the air like loose spiral notebook paper. The money floated to the ground, landing on top of the shooters, soaking up some of their blood.

Right after, gunshots rang from inside of the stash house. Jabari's head whipped toward the house, where he saw silhouettes moving back and forth across the windows. He could hear Jibbs howling in pain and then bitching about being shot.

"Bitch-ass nigga gon' pop my muthafuckin' nigga, huh? Well, eat slugs!" he overheard Spank say, followed by gunshots.

Blocka! Blocka! Blocka! Blocka!

"Yo, grab the loot! I'm going in!" Jabari shouted to Ramone. Sankeesy, who was frozen by fear, frowned upon hearing his voice. The voice sounded familiar, but she couldn't quite put her finger on who it belonged to. Then it suddenly hit her, and her eyes bucked with awareness.

"Ja-Jabari?" Sankeesy said his name like she wasn't sure it was him.

Jabari was halfway up the steps when he heard his name. He turned around and upped his shotgun. His heart sank when he locked eyes with Sankeesy and recalled who she was: Sanka's cousin. Sankeesy became queasy when realizing she was in grave danger.

Sankeesy swallowed the lump of terror in her throat and took off running. Jabari switched hands with his shotgun and chased after her. He knew if he wasn't able to stop her, then his ass would be fertilizer. Sanka would spare no expense to find him and make him pay for his sins. His only chance was to snatch up Sankeesy before she could get away and report to her cousin what happened.

Jabari ran past Ramone, who was busy stuffing the duffle bags the blue faces had spilled out of. Sankeesy had cleared the threshold out of the yard with Jabari on her heels. She occasionally glanced over her shoulder at him, screaming and hollering for help. Jabari swept one of her feet out from under her and she slammed face first into the sidewalk. Her mouth exploded in blood and broken teeth. She peeled her face up from the ground, seeing double and spitting blood and teeth fragments.

Jabari racked his shotgun and pressed it to the back of her wig. He was about to knock her head off, but something else came to mind.

Naw, I'm not gon' body this bitch. I'ma hold on to her ass and use her as leverage to get some birds up outta Sanka. When he finds out I got his cousin, he'll be willin' to gimme anything I want.

Jabari grabbed Sankeesy under her arm and pulled her up roughly. He led her back to the Astro van, snatched open the door, and shoved her inside with the dopefiend. The old dopefiend climbed from out of the driver's seat with a nickel-plated .44 magnum revolver, swatting the flies circling his funky ass.

"Gag, bag, and tie this bitch up," Jabari ordered him.

"You've got it, boss." The dopefiend nodded, tucking his pistol in the small of his back. He grabbed a bandana and a zip-tie and carried out the task he was given.

Jabari turned around to the stash house, where he found Ramone with both duffle bags of Sanka's money. Spank held Jibbs' arm around his shoulders as he helped him down the steps. Jibbs limped beside him with a bandana tied around his wounded leg. Jabari gathered he'd gotten popped in the leg during the gun battle inside the stash house.

"Grrrrrrrr! This shit hurt like a bitch, son. Word to mine," Jibbs swore, holding a warm gun in his gloved hand.

"You good, my G?" Jabari asked Jibbs.

"Yeah." Jibbs winced.

"Good." Jabari turned to Ramone, who'd loaded the duffle bags in the van. "Come on, King, you gon' help me with the rest of these bags," he told him as he rifled through the shooters' pockets until he came up with the keys to the Chevrolet Suburban.

Police car sirens wailed in the distance as Jabari and Ramone loaded their van with the duffle bags from the truck. They then jumped into the back of the van, shut the door, and disappeared into the night.

***

Jabari hit the old dopefiend with two gees as promised and dropped him off on the corner. He then drove to an old house with boarded-up windows and dead grass. It used to be a sanctuary for junkies to get high and get a good night's sleep, but Jabari and his demons took the necessary actions to claim it as theirs. Jabari parked in the backyard and everyone hopped out. Ramone was last as he was attending to Sankeesy. She was blindfolded, gagged, and her wrists were bound behind her. Ramone kept his gun in her back while leading her to the back door. He kept an eye on his surroundings as he waited for Jabari to unlock the backdoor.

"Home sweet home," Jabari said, opening the back door. He took a lighter from his pocket and started lighting the candles scattered around in the kitchen. The sudden appearance of the candles flames caused roaches to crawl and mice to scatter. "Y'all start splitting this shit up. I'll take shorty down into the basement," he told them as he emptied the duffle bags of their spoils on the kitchen table and slung them aside.

Jabari grabbed Sankeesy by her arm and picked up one of the candles. He opened the basement door and led her down the staircase with the light of his candle leading the way. He made her stand by the staircase while he took the time to light the candles scattered around inside of the basement. He set his candle aside, tied Sankeesy to a chair, and took out her cell phone. He scrolled the call log until he came upon Sanka's name. He pulled the gag down from out of her mouth as the telephone rang.

"Shhhhh." Jabari held his finger to his lips. Sankeesy's makeup had run from her crying and she was trembling fearfully. "Relax, li'l baby. Long as yo' punk-ass cousin gives me what I want, we're all good. You can walk up out this bitch a free woman. I promise," he lied as he stroked the side of her face with the back of his hand.

She jerked her face away from his hand and spat in his face. He wiped her spit up with his thumb, looked at it, and sucked it off. He smiled at her wickedly and then backhand slapped her ass. She yelped and hung her head. Right after, Sanka answered the call. Jabari placed a voice distortion device on the end of his jack and started talking to him.

Chapter 21

Every exercise machine known to man – barbells, dumbbells, a shower room, a sauna, a basketball court, and a sixty-inch flat screen on all four walls - made up Sanka's home gymnasium.

Sweat poured down his face, chest and back as he jumped rope at a fast pace. The sound of the rope whistling through the air and clashing against the floor below him filled the air.

Hearing his cell phone ringing, Sanka wrapped up his exercising and hung the rope around his neck. He snatched up a towel, dabbing his face dry and wiping the sweat from his glistening body. He picked up his iPhone, put on the Bluetooth headset, and answered the call.

"Sankeesy, I take it everything went as planned." Sanka asked, sitting down on the bench and wiping away the sweat above his lip.

"Yep. We managed to snatch this bitch up for a payday," the caller spoke with a creepy distorted voice that gave Sanka cause for concern.

Sanka's brows wrinkled and he stood up. "I don't know who this is, but if this is your idea of a joke, I'm definitely not the one you wanna——"

"Nigga, shut cho Spear chuckin' ass up. This ain't no muthafuckin' joke. Niggas ain't playing wit'cho ass." the caller assured him. "Check this out, if you want this bitch back in one piece, then it's gon' cost you."

"Oh, yeah? Well, gimme a number."

"Two thousand."

"Two thousand dollars? You went through all of this trouble for——"

"Nah, muthafucka, not two geez, two thousand bricks of Rebirth by tomorrow night."

"You've gotta be fuckin' kiddin' me. I can't get my hands on that much product in such a——"

Bocka!

Sankeesy's screams erupted through the telephone.

"Sankeesy? Sankeesy? Are you there? Speak to me!" a terrified Sanka hollered into the telephone.

"Relax, my boy. She may have lost the hearing in her left ear, but she'll live," the caller assured him. "Niggas hadda let chu know we ain't playin' wit'chu. If you tell me somethin' other than you gon' have my work by tomorrow night, I'ma shoot shorty right in her face."

Sanka was so hot you could fry an egg on his head sunny side up. He squared his jaws, flared his nostrils, and balled his fist so tight his knuckles cracked. "You'll have your shipment by tomorrow night."

"Good. We'll be in contact to let chu know the time and location." The caller hung up before Sanka could get in another word.

Overcome by rage, Sanka grabbed a 35 pound dumbbell and hurled it across the gym. The mirror cracked into a spider's cobweb and left Sanka staring at several distorted images of himself.

***

After Jabari hung up from talking to Sanka, he sat Sankeesy back up in her chair and placed the gag in her mouth. He tucked his banger in his waistband and turned around to the staircase. Spank, Jibbs, and Ramone were standing on it looking around with their guns at their sides. They'd heard the shot that Jabari fired to get Sanka's attention in the kitchen and thought niggas had rushed the spot.

"Fuck's going on, bro?" Spank asked.

"Shit. Just hadda get shorty's cousin's attention." Jabari told them. "Y'all finished dividing up that take?"

Spank nodded. "Yeah. We were just about to come down here and get chu when we heard that gunshot."

"Cool," Jabari replied.

"So, what homie say?" Ramone asked.

Jabari smiled and rubbed his hands together greedily. "My niggas, ya boy just came up on two thousand of them thangs. And they're set to drop tomorrow night."

Ramone and them whistled at the sound of getting two thousand birds of Rebirth dropped on them. Once they sold all of that shit, they were going to be looking at some major chips.

"Spank and Jibbs, I want y'all to pick it up at the drop zone. It's gonna be at the same spot we trained the young'un here," Jabari referred to Ramone as he headed up the staircase with his savage animals following behind him.

"Fa sho, Blood. We got chu faded," Jibbs assured him, dapping up Spank as they entered the kitchen.

"What's my role in alla this, Dunn?" Ramone asked, tucking his piece in his waistband.

Jabari turned around to him, cupping his face and looking him in his eyes. "You get what you always wanted: the muthafucka that crushed yo' big bruh. I'm gonna give you the spot he lays low at. The only person that knows this location is me, him, and his brother. But chu don't have to worry about the big homie 'cause he's locked up indefinitely."

"I appreciate that, but I've been thinking, son," Ramone said, standing beside Jibbs and Spank, loading his cut from the licks they hit inside of his knapsack. "I don't wanna just run up on this nigga and do 'em. I want to come at him face to face and gun this shit out."

"My nigga, you've got some set of balls on you. And I admire that shit, straight up," Jabari told him. "I tell you what.

139

If you don't want 'em gift wrapped and waiting for you, then you have my blessing to handle yo' bidness with a showdown. You just make sure you stop that nigga from existing." He pointed his finger at his chest.

"My word," Ramone replied, slipping the knapsack over his shoulder. He dapped up Jabari and gave him a thug hug. He then dapped up Spank and Jibbs and left.

***

Olivia and Paperchase made out under the spraying hot water of the showerhead. The water flowed down their bodies, rinsing the soap suds down the drain. Paperchase lathered a loofah and washed her from head to toe. Once he was finished, she did the same, placing gentle kisses down the small of his back. Tilting his head back, he closed his eyes and gasped, feeling her grab his flaccid penis and begin pumping it. She nibbled on his earlobe while she continued to pump his piece, feeling it grow wider and longer in her hand. She placed her foot on the edge of the tub and flicked her clit rapidly with her ring finger. Their moaning married and created a symphony with the sound of the flowing shower water.

Olivia heard her cell phone ringing as Paperchase grunted and bucked. He shuddered while spewing rope after rope of his hot, gooey babies onto the shower wall. Olivia, with her eyes closed and the side of her face smashed against his back, shrieked in pleasure. Her body was racked by one hell of an orgasm. Her entire body shivered like she was naked in 30°-below weather.

Olivia kept the side of her face against Paperchase's back while holding his waist. Her breathing was labored and her legs were shaking. A smile spread across her face, thinking of how great the orgasm she experienced was. Paperchase reached over his shoulder and grabbed the back of her head. He kissed her hungrily while the water continued to flow over their faces and bodies.

Olivia's cell phone started ringing for what seemed like the millionth time that night.

"Damn, you're popular tonight, shorty. Yo' jack ringing off the hook."

"That's probably the girls again, trying to see what's holding me up."

"Tell 'em you were helping yo' man relieve some stress."

"Shiiit, if I tell them that and it gets back to yo' brother, the cops will find us both somewhere stretched out with bullets in our heads. Ya heard?" Olivia told him, holding the shower curtain while standing halfway out of the tub.

"I ain't afraid of shit but Jesus, li'l baby."

"Oh, I love me a thug-ass nigga."

Olivia grinned, pulled him close and kissed him again. When she turned around to leave, he smacked her on her ass. She snatched a towel off the rack, wrapped it around her bosom, and sauntered down the hallway toward her ringing cellular. When she saw it was S, she rolled her eyes and answered the call.

"This is so not the time for you to be calling me," Olivia said in a hushed tone, glancing over her shoulder to make sure Paperchase wasn't around. "No, I haven't. It isn't that easy, Sanka. A bitch done developed feelings for this ni——I mean, dude," she corrected herself remembering how much he hated the N-word being thrown around in his presence. "You wouldn't dare, especially while I'm carrying your unborn child."

"You think the fact that my child's growing inside of you buys you some immunity from my wrath? If so, beloved, let me remind you when it comes to my business, I couldn't give

Ghost & Tranay Adams

a fuck about you or that child," Sanka told her. "I assure you, I can find a woman far more suitable to carry my seed."

Olivia turned around from looking over her shoulder again, focusing her attention on the call. "What? I don't know who the fuck you think you're talking to, bro, but I'm not the one. Nigga, suck my big black dick!"

"What?" Sanka replied heatedly.

"You heard me, you mud hut building piece of shit!" Olivia went in on him. "I'm an American, a woman from a first world country. We don't bow down to niggas like them bitches over there in Nigeria." Olivia waited for his response, but it never came. He'd hung up. "Hello? Hello?"

Olivia gasped, seeing someone at the corner of her eye. She looked over her shoulder, but there wasn't anyone there. She set her cell phone down on the nightstand and peeked out of the doorway. There wasn't anyone there either. She looked up and down the hallway and it was empty as well. She could hear the shower water still running, so she decided to check the bathroom. She saw Paperchase washing up and reciting the lyrics to a 22Gz song. He abruptly looked in her direction.

"Liv?" Paperchase inquired.

Olivia cleared her throat before answering him. "Yeah."

"So who was that?"

"My cousin Blanca rushing me. I told you."

"Word? That's what's up," he told her. "Well, I'ma just kick it here until you get back. It's been a while since a nigga had time to chill."

"What chu gon' do?"

"Probably chief one and watch some old gangsta flicks."

"A'ight. Well, I'm finna go get ready for tonight. Love you," she told him.

"Love you too, ma."

"More than you love our baby?"

142

"Hell nah. I don't love nobody more than I love my unborn, for real, for real. I'ma spoil the shit outta my li'l nigga whenever they get here."

"How the fuck you know it's gonna be a boy?"

"Willpower, shorty. It's all in the mind." Paperchase tapped his finger against his temple.

"Yeah. A'ight." Olivia chuckled as she walked out of the bathroom.

Ghost & Tranay Adams

Chapter 22

Toya was sitting on the couch painting her toenails when she heard the front door unlock. She pulled her gun from where it was wedged between the couch's cushions and called out to Ramone. When she upped her gun to shoot the possible intruder, the front door swung open and Ramone stepped inside. A look of relief came across Toya's face and she lowered her gun.

"Bae, you didn't hear me calling your name? I was about to start busting," Toya told him. "I didn't know who it was coming through that door."

"Shorty, who else could it possibly be with a key?" Ramone held up his house key.

"True. But with alla the shit we're involved in, you never know what's gon' pop off. Now gimme a kiss." She threw her arms around his neck and kissed him like a wife would her husband coming home after long hours at the office. "Damn, bae, you smell like weed and alcohol." she said, catching a whiff of his scent. She looked at the two duffle bags in his hands and then at his Timbs. There were dots of dried blood on the toes of both of them.

"I thought you boys were just going to grab a few shots and watch some hoes shake some ass. What's this?" She pointed down at the blood on his boots.

Ramone looked down at the crimson stains on his Trees. "Ma, to answer alla your future questions about shit like this, anytime you see me with blood on my shoes it's from one of two thangs. One, I ran into a nigga I got static with and we banged it out. Two, I was out making moves to net me a bag." He set the duffle bags on the kitchen table. He watched her unzip both of the bags while he removed his jacket and hung it on the back of the chair.

"Damn, how much is this?" Toya inquired.

Ramone took her in his arms. "Like a hunnit and fiddy bands. That's not including that bird of raw in there." Toya, holding five ten thousand dollar stacks in each hand, threw her arms around his neck and kissed him again. "You thought about that business we discussed?"

Before Ramone had left the crib, he proposed that they take over her father's drug operation. Toya, on the other hand, wanted to sell the kilos at a wholesale price to this nigga she knew Uptown. Since little mama knew the ins and outs of her father's business, Ramone felt that she should handle the logistics side of things while he played the role of enforcer. He only hoped the workers were on board because it would save them the time of having to assemble a new street team.

"Yeah. And I'm with it." Toya smiled, tucking the blue cheese back inside of the duffle bag.

"Cool. We can use this loot to move the fuck up outta here and get the necessities," Ramone told her. "Yo, ma, I'm tryna squash this shit with yo' boy tonight."

"With who? Maurice?" Ramone nodded. "You mean you letting 'em slide?"

Ramone frowned. "Fuck naw. This beef ain't over 'til his bitch ass is dead. That's on gang."

Toya put her hand on her hip and switched her weight to her other foot. "So what do you propose?"

"You gimme that fool's math so I can set it up for us to meet up and let these guns resolve our issue."

"I hear you, babe, but don't chu think it would be better to catch dude slipping?"

"Nah, ma, it's gotta be done this way. This nigga gotta know that when we clashed, I was the better man. Ya smell me?" Toya nodded. "Good. You got my back?"

"Boy, I got cho front, back and both your sides," she assured him.

"That's why you're my ride or die." He stared deep into her eyes and they made out. "Look here, I'ma go take a shower then I'ma holla at this nigga to see where he's at with it."

"Okay."

"You still got his math, right?"

Toya nodded. "Gimme yo' clothes so I can get rid of 'em."

Ramone stripped down naked and handed his pile of clothes to Toya. He kissed her and turned to head for the bathroom. She smacked his ass as he walked past her, admiring his physique.

***

Since all the kingpins' girlfriends, wives and fiancées had upheld their end of the agreement, Olivia called for the second meeting so they could discuss their next move.

Echo carried out her assignment with the knife and gun Olivia had given her. These were the same knife and gun Paperchase used to kill Blake and his wife. Having been sidetracked, he had given the murder weapons to Olivia to dispose of for him. Unbeknownst to him, shorty had devised a plan with Echo to get her kingpin of a baby daddy Devonte out of the way since she couldn't bring herself to kill his ass. The plan was for her to frame him for the murders and put him away for a very long time.

Though Echo had agreed to go along with the plan, she found it difficult to go through with when the time presented itself. It took her thinking back to all the shit that no good, trifling nigga did to her for her to complete the task. She waited until Devonte had fallen asleep, slipped on a pair of latex gloves and wrapped his hands around the handles of the murder weapons, insuring his fingerprints were on them.

Echo stashed the knife and gun in places she was going to tell Jake to look when they arrived at their home. Once she'd stashed the weapons in their hiding places, she beat herself black and blue and called 9-1-1. Devonte woke up from them banging on the front door and shouting demands. Echo answered the door looking like she'd been to hell and back, sold the police a bogus story she'd cooked up, and the rest was history.

When Echo pulled up outside of Cruzito's establishment, she noticed that she was the last one to arrive. Blanca was standing outside the entrance of the bar wearing the same attire she had been the first time all the girls had met up. Echo turned off her car, slid on her oversized designer shades, and hopped out of her BMW. She exchanged pleasantries with Bubbles and her chauffeur/bodyguard, Martin. Blanca stopped them at the entrance of the bar. She looked Martin up and down, wondering what the fuck he was doing there.

"This li'l shindig is ladies only, homeboy," Blanca said and then extended her retractable baton in case Martin wanted to smoke.

"I know," Bubbles replied, directing her attention towards her. "He has to use the men's room then he'll be gon' 'bout his business, sis."

Blanca thought things over as she took a close look at Martin. He stood there with a solemn face and his hands at his sides. "A'ight, y'all can come in, but after I frisk his big ass. Assume the position, white boy," she ordered with a sway of her finger. Martin turned his back to her, sliding his legs apart and outstretching his arms. Blanca gave him a thorough pat down that produced a big-ass Desert Eagle. She tested its weight, then stuck it in the small of her back. "You'll get this blicky back on your way out," she told him. She then patted the ladies down and allowed them inside behind Martin.

Blanca scanned the area before ducking back inside of Cruzito's, slamming and locking the door behind her. Unfortunately, she didn't spot the Nigerians sitting in the Mercedes-Benz 600 a block away. They had been watching the spot since Olivia and Blanca showed up. The one that had planted the bomb inside of the bar sat in the front passenger seat with the detonator in his hands. He pulled up the antenna of the device, flipped a couple of switches on it, and lifted the see-through covering that covered the red detonation button.

Together, the Nigerians counted down lifting a finger as they did so, "Three, two, one!"

Ka-Boom!

The explosion rocked the entire area and set off the alarms of cars parked up and down the block. The Nigerians smiled and bumped fists. The Nigerian in the driver seat cranked up the Mercedes, pulled away from the curb, and drove past Cruzito's bar. The reflection of the establishment shone on the passenger window as the Nigerian riding shotgun looked up at it proudly. He watched as smoke slowly began to rise from the shady business. Having seen enough, he pulled out his burnout cellular and hit up his boss.

***

Sanka, dressed in his red silk pajamas, sat on his throne stroking a lion cub. An incoming call garnered his attention. Seeing it was the Nigerians he'd sent to handle a very important task for him, he adjusted his Bluetooth and answered the call.

"Hello?" Sanka spoke into the telephone.

"Happy birthday, boss." the Nigerian replied.

"So glad to hear from you, thank you so much." Sanka smiled.

Fuckin' half-bred bitch, that'll teach chu to speak to royalty in such a manor, Sanka thought as he disconnected the call. The smile on his face was replaced with a more serious one. He placed another call for what would be one of the biggest shipments of Rebirth he had acquired in all of his years in the dope game.

Chapter 23

Paperchase was as angry as bees in a hive being swatted by a stick. He'd definitely heard Olivia's conversation with whomever she was talking to and it made him sick to his fucking stomach. Shorty had played him for a fucking chump and to add insult to injury, the bitch planned on bodying him after she was done with him. He was both angry and hurt because he really did love shorty. He saw a future with her he never saw with any bitch he fucked with.

That's what my black ass get, son. I didn't have no business fucking with big bro's bitch, so I rightfully deserve whatever this ho got lined up for me, Paperchase thought as he stood before the medicine cabinet mirror brushing his teeth. His gun was lying on the porcelain sink right beside the soap dispenser. *I'm not going out like a sucka though. I'ma give it to shorty and whoever this buster-ass nigga is that's supposed to be her baby daddy. When I catch up with them they're gon' feel a gangsta's pain, real talk.*

Paperchase's cell phone had been ringing nonstop. He checked to see who was calling a few times before he went to the bathroom and every time it was a blocked call, so he didn't answer it. He considered turning it off but it was his personal number and everyone he had mad love for had it.

"Goddamn, Blood, you a persistent muthafucka!" Paperchase said, agitated as he picked up his cellphone and answered it. "Fucks up? Damn!"

"What's up is you and me linkin' up tonight to settle this beef once and for all," Ramone replied with a dangerous edge to his voice. The young nigga was in full demon mode and ready to wild the fuck out.

"Yo, who the fuck is this?" Paperchase asked, walking aimlessly around his bedroom.

"The nigga that was bustin' at cho ho-ass the other night."

"The white boy?"

"You's a whole bitch, son. You got that many niggas tryna blow yo' shit back?"

"Yo, what the fuck is this shit all about? Why you got a problem with me?"

Ramone got as hot as fish grease then. "Nigga, don't play fuckin' stupid with me! You know exactly what this shit is about, and it ain't ending until yo' ass lying somewhere stankin', word to Jayshawn."

"Wait. This Ramone?" A confused look crossed Paperchase's face. "Young King, you think I got somethin' to do with what happened to yo' fam?"

"I hear you, my nigga. You's a real fuckin' goofy. But check this fly shit out, bruh: 'less you wanna spend the rest of yo' life duckin' and dodgin' bullets, I suggest you strap up and meet me alone at this address..." Ramone gave Paperchase the address.

He searched through envelopes and loose papers until he found something to write on. He grabbed an ink pen, snatched the top off with his teeth, and quickly jotted down the location and time.

"The last man standin' wins. Good luck, fuck nigga." Ramone hung up.

Paperchase looked at his cell phone like *the nerve of this little nigga* before pocketing it.

A'ight, li'l homie. We're on demon time now. You wanna play with the guns? Well, we're gonna play all night long, Paperchase thought while strapping on a white bulletproof-vest and slipping a sweatshirt over his head. He made sure both his FN's were fully loaded and tucked them in his waistband. He slipped on his puffy jacket and pulled his beanie over his head, adjusting it to his liking.

***

Ramone, who was dressed in all black, hung up on Paper-chase and set his cell phone on the kitchen table. He picked up a rolled up $100 dollar bill and tooted up the lines of cocaine laid out in front of him. He rubbed the cocaine residue across his gums and made an ugly face. That shit was so potent it had his entire face and mouth numb.

"What that nigga say, boo?" Toya asked from the other side of the table, where she was adjusting the sighting on her M24. She was wearing a black hoodie and black bandana.

"He's with it," Ramone replied, loading bullets into the magazines of his bangers. His eyes were glassy and red-webbed and snot peeked out of his right nostril. The facial hair he'd grown made him look much older than his sixteen years.

"Told you Dunn hadda ego. There wasn't no way in hell he was gon' turn you down," Toya told him, looking through the scope of her military-issued sniper rifle.

Ramone finished loading up and click clacking them thangs and tucked them in his waistband. He pulled a black skully over his short dreadlocks and walked over to Toya. She'd just closed the lid on the carrying case of the sniper rifle and picked it up by its handle.

Ramone glanced at his digital timepiece and looked back up at her. "We better roll out now so we can get there early to set up on this fool." Toya nodded understandingly. "Remember, if I come out on the losing end of this thing, you make sure this muthafucka goes down for good. A nigga soul we'll never rest peacefully knowing he's still alive after smokin' my bro."

"I'm not worried about you coming out on the losing end, baby," she said, caressing the side of his face affectionately.

"Yo' Glizzies are laced with armor piercing rounds so even if this nigga is rockin' a vest, it ain't gon' do 'em no good."

"I know. I'm just sayin', yo, in case shit doesn't go as planned."

"Understood. I love you, Ramone."

"I love you too, shorty. You're the only reason a nigga hasn't joined big bro up there."

They kissed, killed the lights, and left the house to see what fate had in store for them.

***

Paperchase sent a prayer up to the Big Man in the sky, asking for the odds to be in his favor that night. He grabbed his keys and opened the front door. His eyes widened when came face to face with an unexpected visitor.

"Surprise! I'm home, li'l bro!" Scorpion smiled.

To Be Continued...
The King of the Trap 3
Coming Soon

Lock Down Publications and Ca$h Presents assisted
publishing packages.

BASIC PACKAGE $499
Editing
Cover Design
Formatting

UPGRADED PACKAGE $800
Typing
Editing
Cover Design
Formatting

ADVANCE PACKAGE $1,200
Typing
Editing
Cover Design
Formatting
Copyright registration
Proofreading
Upload book to Amazon

LDP SUPREME PACKAGE $1,500
Typing
Editing
Cover Design
Formatting
Copyright registration
Proofreading
Set up Amazon account
Upload book to Amazon
Advertise on LDP Amazon and Facebook page

***Other services available upon request. Additional
charges may apply
**Lock Down Publications
P.O. Box 944
Stockbridge, GA 30281-9998
Phone # 470 303-9761**

Submission Guideline

Submit the first three chapters of your completed manuscript to ldpsubmissions@gmail.com, subject line: Your book's title. The manuscript must be in a .doc file and sent as an attachment. Document should be in Times New Roman, double spaced and in size 12 font. Also, provide your synopsis and full contact information. If sending multiple submissions, they must each be in a separate email.

Have a story but no way to send it electronically? You can still submit to LDP/Ca$h Presents. Send in the first three chapters, written or typed, of your completed manuscript to:

LDP: Submissions Dept
Po Box 944
Stockbridge, Ga 30281

DO NOT send original manuscript. Must be a duplicate.

Provide your synopsis and a cover letter containing your full contact information.

Thanks for considering LDP and Ca$h Presents.

<u>NEW RELEASES</u>

A GANGSTA SAVED XMAS by MONET DRA-
GUN
XMAS WITH AN ATL SHOOTER by CA$H &
DESTINY SKAI
CUM FOR ME by SUGAR E. WALLZ
THE BRICK MAN 3 by KING RIO
THE PLUG OF LIL MEXICO by CHRIS
GREEN
THE STREETS STAINED MY SOUL 3 by
MARCELLUS ALLEN
KING OF THE TRENCHES 2 by GHOST &
TRANAY ADAMS

Coming Soon from Lock Down Publications/Ca$h Presents
BLOOD OF A BOSS **VI**
SHADOWS OF THE GAME II
TRAP BASTARD II
By **Askari**
LOYAL TO THE GAME **IV**
By **T.J. & Jelissa**
IF TRUE SAVAGE **VIII**
MIDNIGHT CARTEL IV
DOPE BOY MAGIC IV
CITY OF KINGZ III
NIGHTMARE ON SILENT AVE II
THE PLUG OF LIL MEXICO II
By **Chris Green**
BLAST FOR ME **III**
A SAVAGE DOPEBOY III
CUTTHROAT MAFIA III
DUFFLE BAG CARTEL VII
HEARTLESS GOON VI
By **Ghost**
A HUSTLER'S DECEIT III
KILL ZONE II
BAE BELONGS TO ME III
By **Aryanna**
KING OF THE TRAP III
By **T.J. Edwards**
GORILLAZ IN THE BAY V
3X KRAZY III
STRAIGHT BEAST MODE II
De'Kari
KINGPIN KILLAZ IV
STREET KINGS III
PAID IN BLOOD III
CARTEL KILLAZ IV
DOPE GODS III
Hood Rich
SINS OF A HUSTLA II
ASAD
RICH $AVAGE II
MONEY IN THE GRAVE II

By Martell Troublesome Bolden
YAYO V
Bred In The Game 2
S. Allen
CREAM III
By Yolanda Moore
SON OF A DOPE FIEND III
HEAVEN GOT A GHETTO II
By Renta
LOYALTY AIN'T PROMISED III
By Keith Williams
I'M NOTHING WITHOUT HIS LOVE II
SINS OF A THUG II
TO THE THUG I LOVED BEFORE II
By Monet Dragun
QUIET MONEY IV
EXTENDED CLIP III
THUG LIFE IV
By **Trai'Quan**
THE STREETS MADE ME IV
By **Larry D. Wright**
IF YOU CROSS ME ONCE II
By **Anthony Fields**
THE STREETS WILL NEVER CLOSE II
By K'ajji
HARD AND RUTHLESS III
THE BILLIONAIRE BENTLEYS II
Von Diesel
KILLA KOUNTY II
By Khufu
MONEY GAME III
By Smoove Dolla
JACK BOYZ VERSUS DOPE BOYZ
By Romell Tukes
MURDA WAS THE CASE II
Elijah R. Freeman
THE STREETS NEVER LET GO II
By Robert Baptiste
AN UNFORESEEN LOVE III
By **Meesha**

KING OF THE TRENCHES III
by **GHOST & TRANAY ADAMS**

MONEY MAFIA II
LOYAL TO THE SOIL II
By **Jibril Williams**
QUEEN OF THE ZOO II
By **Black Migo**
THE BRICK MAN IV
By King Rio
VICIOUS LOYALTY II
By Kingpen
A GANGSTA'S PAIN II
By J-Blunt
CONFESSIONS OF A JACKBOY III
By Nicholas Lock
GRIMEY WAYS II
By Ray Vinci

Available Now

RESTRAINING ORDER **I & II**
By **CA$H & Coffee**
LOVE KNOWS NO BOUNDARIES **I II & III**
By **Coffee**
RAISED AS A GOON I, II, III & IV
BRED BY THE SLUMS I, II, III
BLAST FOR ME I & II
ROTTEN TO THE CORE I II III
A BRONX TALE I, II, III
DUFFLE BAG CARTEL I II III IV V VI
HEARTLESS GOON I II III IV V
A SAVAGE DOPEBOY I II
DRUG LORDS I II III

CUTTHROAT MAFIA I II
KING OF THE TRENCHES
By **Ghost**
LAY IT DOWN **I & II**
LAST OF A DYING BREED I II
BLOOD STAINS OF A SHOTTA I & II III
By **Jamaica**
LOYAL TO THE GAME I II III
LIFE OF SIN I, II III
By **TJ & Jelissa**
BLOODY COMMAS I & II
SKI MASK CARTEL I II & III
KING OF NEW YORK I II,III IV V
RISE TO POWER I II III
COKE KINGS I II III IV V
BORN HEARTLESS I II III IV
KING OF THE TRAP I II
By **T.J. Edwards**
IF LOVING HIM IS WRONG…I & II
LOVE ME EVEN WHEN IT HURTS I II III
By **Jelissa**
WHEN THE STREETS CLAP BACK I & II III
THE HEART OF A SAVAGE I II III
MONEY MAFIA
LOYAL TO THE SOIL
By **Jibril Williams**
A DISTINGUISHED THUG STOLE MY HEART I II & III
LOVE SHOULDN'T HURT I II III IV
RENEGADE BOYS I II III IV
PAID IN KARMA I II III
SAVAGE STORMS I II
AN UNFORESEEN LOVE I II
By **Meesha**
A GANGSTER'S CODE I &, II III
A GANGSTER'S SYN I II III
THE SAVAGE LIFE I II III
CHAINED TO THE STREETS I II III
BLOOD ON THE MONEY I II III
A GANGSTA'S PAIN
By J-Blunt

PUSH IT TO THE LIMIT
By **Bre' Hayes**
BLOOD OF A BOSS **I, II, III, IV, V**
SHADOWS OF THE GAME
TRAP BASTARD
By **Askari**
THE STREETS BLEED MURDER **I, II & III**
THE HEART OF A GANGSTA I II& III
By **Jerry Jackson**
CUM FOR ME I II III IV V VI VII VIII
An **LDP Erotica Collaboration**
BRIDE OF A HUSTLA **I II & II**
THE FETTI GIRLS **I, II& III**
CORRUPTED BY A GANGSTA I, II III, IV
BLINDED BY HIS LOVE
THE PRICE YOU PAY FOR LOVE I, II ,III
DOPE GIRL MAGIC I II III
By **Destiny Skai**
WHEN A GOOD GIRL GOES BAD
By **Adrienne**
THE COST OF LOYALTY I II III
By Kweli
A GANGSTER'S REVENGE **I II III & IV**
THE BOSS MAN'S DAUGHTERS I II III IV V
A SAVAGE LOVE **I & II**
BAE BELONGS TO ME I II
A HUSTLER'S DECEIT I, II, III
WHAT BAD BITCHES DO I, II, III
SOUL OF A MONSTER I II III
KILL ZONE
A DOPE BOY'S QUEEN I II III
By **Aryanna**
A KINGPIN'S AMBITON
A KINGPIN'S AMBITION **II**
I MURDER FOR THE DOUGH
By **Ambitious**
TRUE SAVAGE I II III IV V VI VII
DOPE BOY MAGIC I, II, III
MIDNIGHT CARTEL I II III
CITY OF KINGZ I II

NIGHTMARE ON SILENT AVE
THE PLUG OF LIL MEXICO II

By **Chris Green**
A DOPEBOY'S PRAYER
By **Eddie "Wolf" Lee**
THE KING CARTEL **I, II & III**
By **Frank Gresham**
THESE NIGGAS AIN'T LOYAL **I, II & III**
By **Nikki Tee**
GANGSTA SHYT **I II &III**
By **CATO**
THE ULTIMATE BETRAYAL
By **Phoenix**
BOSS'N UP **I , II & III**
By **Royal Nicole**
I LOVE YOU TO DEATH
By **Destiny J**
I RIDE FOR MY HITTA
I STILL RIDE FOR MY HITTA
By **Misty Holt**
LOVE & CHASIN' PAPER
By **Qay Crockett**
TO DIE IN VAIN
SINS OF A HUSTLA
By **ASAD**
BROOKLYN HUSTLAZ
By **Boogsy Morina**
BROOKLYN ON LOCK I & II
By **Sonovia**
GANGSTA CITY
By **Teddy Duke**
A DRUG KING AND HIS DIAMOND I & II III
A DOPEMAN'S RICHES
HER MAN, MINE'S TOO I, II
CASH MONEY HO'S
THE WIFEY I USED TO BE I II
By Nicole Goosby
TRAPHOUSE KING **I II & III**
KINGPIN KILLAZ I II III

STREET KINGS I II
PAID IN BLOOD **I II**
CARTEL KILLAZ I II III
DOPE GODS I II
By **Hood Rich**
LIPSTICK KILLAH **I, II, III**
CRIME OF PASSION I II & III
FRIEND OR FOE I II III
By **Mimi**
STEADY MOBBN' **I, II, III**
THE STREETS STAINED MY SOUL I II III
By **Marcellus Allen**
WHO SHOT YA **I, II, III**
SON OF A DOPE FIEND I II
HEAVEN GOT A GHETTO
Renta
GORILLAZ IN THE BAY **I II III IV**
TEARS OF A GANGSTA I II
3X KRAZY I II
STRAIGHT BEAST MODE
DE'KARI
TRIGGADALE I II III
MURDAROBER WAS THE CASE
Elijah R. Freeman
GOD BLESS THE TRAPPERS I, II, III
THESE SCANDALOUS STREETS I, II, III
FEAR MY GANGSTA I, II, III IV, V
THESE STREETS DON'T LOVE NOBODY I, II
BURY ME A G I, II, III, IV, V
A GANGSTA'S EMPIRE I, II, III, IV
THE DOPEMAN'S BODYGAURD I II
THE REALEST KILLAZ I II III
THE LAST OF THE OGS I II III
Tranay Adams
THE STREETS ARE CALLING
Duquie Wilson
MARRIED TO A BOSS I II III
By Destiny Skai & Chris Green
KINGZ OF THE GAME I II III IV V VI
Playa Ray

SLAUGHTER GANG I II III
RUTHLESS HEART I II III
By Willie Slaughter
FUK SHYT
By Blakk Diamond
DON'T F#CK WITH MY HEART I II
By Linnea
ADDICTED TO THE DRAMA I II III
IN THE ARM OF HIS BOSS II
By Jamila
YAYO I II III IV
A SHOOTER'S AMBITION I II
BRED IN THE GAME
By S. Allen
TRAP GOD I II III
RICH $AVAGE
MONEY IN THE GRAVE I II
By Martell Troublesome Bolden
FOREVER GANGSTA
GLOCKS ON SATIN SHEETS I II
By Adrian Dulan
TOE TAGZ I II III
LEVELS TO THIS SHYT I II
By Ah'Million
KINGPIN DREAMS I II III
By Paper Boi Rari
CONFESSIONS OF A GANGSTA I II III IV
CONFESSIONS OF A JACKBOY I II
By Nicholas Lock
I'M NOTHING WITHOUT HIS LOVE
SINS OF A THUG
TO THE THUG I LOVED BEFORE
A GANGSTA SAVED XMAS
By Monet Dragun
CAUGHT UP IN THE LIFE I II III
THE STREETS NEVER LET GO
By Robert Baptiste
NEW TO THE GAME I II III
MONEY, MURDER & MEMORIES I II III
By **Malik D. Rice**

LIFE OF A SAVAGE I II III
A GANGSTA'S QUR'AN I II III
MURDA SEASON I II III
GANGLAND CARTEL I II III
CHI'RAQ GANGSTAS I II III
KILLERS ON ELM STREET I II III
JACK BOYZ N DA BRONX I II III
A DOPEBOY'S DREAM I II III
By **Romell Tukes**
LOYALTY AIN'T PROMISED I II
By Keith Williams
QUIET MONEY I II III
THUG LIFE I II III
EXTENDED CLIP I II
By **Trai'Quan**
THE STREETS MADE ME I II III
By **Larry D. Wright**
THE ULTIMATE SACRIFICE I, II, III, IV, V, VI
KHADIFI
IF YOU CROSS ME ONCE
ANGEL I II
IN THE BLINK OF AN EYE
By **Anthony Fields**
THE LIFE OF A HOOD STAR
By Ca$h & Rashia Wilson
THE STREETS WILL NEVER CLOSE
By K'ajji
CREAM I II
By Yolanda Moore
NIGHTMARES OF A HUSTLA I II III
By King Dream
CONCRETE KILLA I II
VICIOUS LOYALTY
By Kingpen
HARD AND RUTHLESS I II
MOB TOWN 251
THE BILLIONAIRE BENTLEYS
By Von Diesel
GHOST MOB
Stilloan Robinson

MOB TIES I II III IV
By SayNoMore
BODYMORE MURDERLAND I II III
By Delmont Player
FOR THE LOVE OF A BOSS
By C. D. Blue
MOBBED UP I II III IV
THE BRICK MAN I II III
By King Rio
KILLA KOUNTY
By Khufu
MONEY GAME I II
By Smoove Dolla
A GANGSTA'S KARMA I II
By FLAME
KING OF THE TRENCHES I II
by **GHOST & TRANAY ADAMS**
QUEEN OF THE ZOO
By **Black Migo**
GRIMEY WAYS
By Ray Vinci
XMAS WITH AN ATL SHOOTER
By Ca$h & Destiny Skai

<u>BOOKS BY LDP'S CEO, CA$H</u>

TRUST IN NO MAN
TRUST IN NO MAN 2
TRUST IN NO MAN 3
BONDED BY BLOOD
SHORTY GOT A THUG
THUGS CRY
THUGS CRY 2
THUGS CRY 3
TRUST NO BITCH
TRUST NO BITCH 2
TRUST NO BITCH 3
TIL MY CASKET DROPS
RESTRAINING ORDER
RESTRAINING ORDER 2
IN LOVE WITH A CONVICT
LIFE OF A HOOD STAR
XMAS WITH AN ATL SHOOTER

CPSIA information can be obtained
at www.ICGtesting.com
Printed in the USA
LVHW082040210522
719400LV00014B/852